PRAISE FOR

THE
LOST
CIPHER

"Oechsle orchestrates a fast-paced narrative that is both poignant and engaging…with ample humor and likable characters."—*School Library Journal*

"There's plenty to like in Oechsle's first novel, including the depiction of Lucas and other well-drawn characters, the treasure hunt, the wilderness adventure…A well-paced story with appealing characters, cliff-hanger moments, and a resonant emotional core."—*Booklist*

"Plenty of humor and heart in this compelling adventure"
—*Publishers Weekly*

THE
LOST
CIPHER

MICHAEL OECHSLE

Albert Whitman & Company
Chicago, Illinois

For Mary Ellen

Library of Congress Cataloging-in-Publication
data is on file with the publisher.

Text copyright © 2016 by Michael Oechsle
Hardcover edition published in 2016 by Albert Whitman & Company
Paperback edition published in 2017 by Albert Whitman & Company
ISBN 978-0-8075-8065-3

Printed in the United States of America
10 9 8 7 6 5 4 3 2 1 BP 22 21 20 19 18 17

Cover illustration by Jorge Monlongo
Design by Jordan Kost

For more information about Albert Whitman & Company,
visit our website at www.albertwhitman.com.

The Beale Ciphers are real, and the lost treasure of Thomas Jefferson Beale may still lie hidden in the Blue Ridge Mountains of Virginia.

The rest of this story is fiction.

"I have deposited in the county of Bedford about four miles from Buford's in an excavation or vault six feet below the surface of the ground the following articles...

"The first deposit consisted of 1,014 pounds of gold and 3,812 pounds of silver deposited November 1819. The second was made December 1821 and consisted of 1,907 pounds of gold and 1,288 pounds of silver...

"Paper number one describes the exact locality of the vault so that no difficulty will be had in finding it."

Words from Thomas Jefferson Beale's second cipher, decoded using the US Declaration of Independence

PROLOGUE

1822, NORTH OF SANTA FE, SPANISH TERRITORY

The first arrow sunk into Beale's leg, nearly taking him down. He grunted in pain but didn't yell out. Instead, he steadied himself and sighted his rifle on the warrior whose arrow now jutted from his thigh. The Indian was galloping away from Beale's desperate stronghold in the rocks, yipping and whooping to the others hidden in the sage, bragging of his skill with a bow. Another arrow pinged off the rock next to Beale's face, sending a tiny shard of its broken point into his cheek. Beale ignored it. He shot the rider squarely in the back of the head, dropping the Apache into the brush.

Beale braced himself against a rock and reloaded, studying the arrow in his leg. He wouldn't try to pull it. If he blacked out from the pain of wrenching the jagged arrowhead from his leg, the Apaches would be on him like wolves. Propping his rifle against a rock, he put a wadded kerchief in his mouth to muffle his scream and snapped the arrow shaft off a couple inches above the skin. Blood flowed a little faster from the wound when he did, but the sudden understanding that he would now die in these lonely rocks filled him with a strange sense of calm.

He considered how close he'd come to the safety of Santa Fe and the chance to live out the rest of his days back in Virginia. Only he and the guide had escaped the canyon. They'd promised the others that help would come and crawled into the frigid creek as soon as the moon set. In the blackest hours of the night, they'd drifted silently past the warriors guarding the canyon mouth. Then, on stolen ponies, they'd set off across the sagebrush, Beale trusting the guide to find the trail along the foot of the Rocky Mountains like he had so many times before.

By the next morning, the guide spotted a moving column of rust-colored dust less than five miles back. They were being hunted.

A hard day and a sleepless night later, the guide stopped next to a jumble of rocks, pulled his rifle and powder from his saddle, and told Beale to ride on. From a mile away, Beale had heard him firing on the Apaches. But when he'd listened again, there was only the wind, and Beale knew his loyal friend had fallen. Now, even Beale's horse was dead, ridden into the ground and shot out of mercy. Only Beale remained.

He looked down at his bloody leg, smiling grimly at the

notion that a few bleached bones scattered across a barren plain, not a handsome grave in a green Virginia field, would be all that remained of Thomas Jefferson Beale.

All except the treasure.

Four tons of gold and silver safely hidden back in the shadow of the Blue Ridge.

When the keys to the codes were delivered, when the old innkeeper finally learned the secrets, at least the wives and children of Beale's men would live like governors for the rest of their lives.

The thought brought him the strength to stand and search the sagebrush for another warrior to kill.

CHAPTER 1

Lucas was down on the rocks by the creek that flowed out of their mountain when the two soldiers came up the road. That's what he remembered now. His grandma had interrupted his schoolwork and sent him out to the garden to see if any rhubarb was worth picking, but he'd been drawn to the creek again—down to where a soft carpet of moss and hemlock needles covered every rock and the sound of water tumbling down through the trees drowned out all the busy sounds of his family's presence in the little hollow under their mountain. Thinking back now, it was almost like he knew that the worst kind of news was coming up their road that morning, like he went down to the creek to keep from hearing it with his own ears.

The creek was the last place Lucas had talked with his pa before he'd gone off to fight again—off to some place so far away and so different from their mountain, from all of West

Virginia even, that Lucas couldn't even dream of what it was like, no matter how many letters his pa wrote or how often the TV showed the treeless, dust-colored country where even the people, scowling men with dark beards and ladies covered head to toe in black, seemed only partly alive.

His pa had taken them up to the head of the hollow, where Lucas's grandma and grandpa lived in their trailer and where Lucas was supposed to stay for the next nine months, maybe more. They'd gone down to the creek that last time, and for a while they hadn't even talked. Just listened to the water and let the sadness hang there, until his pa had tried to explain one more time why going off to be a soldier again was for the best, at least in the long run.

Then his pa had told him to watch over everything for the next nine months. It had been years since his grandpa could get around like normal, ever since the accident in the mine. Now with his pa gone, it would be up to Lucas to help his grandma tend to the garden and keep the truck running or patch up whatever needed fixing around the old trailer, because something always needed fixing. And in April, his father told him, Lucas could go up the mountain on his own for the first time and bring back a spring turkey for the table. He should have felt proud about that, but since there was nothing he loved more in the world than hunting up on the mountain with his pa, he'd mostly just been sad.

And on their way back to the trailer, when they'd cleared the music of the water and heard the dull and far-off rumble of another green mountain crumbling for coal, his pa had told him, only half joking, to take care of their mountain too.

He was remembering those words when he'd come up out of the creek that terrible day and heard the dogs barking like they only did when strangers came up into Indian Hole. By the time Lucas rounded the trailer, the two soldiers were already back at their truck.

But Lucas knew.

One of the soldiers saw him, must have seen the life flowing out of him there at the edge of the woods, because he stopped getting into the truck and said something. Lucas couldn't actually hear the soldier's words over the racket of the dogs and his grandma's sobbing from up on the porch, but they were pretty clear just the same.

"I'm sorry, son."

Except right there and then, Lucas knew he wasn't anyone's son anymore.

CHAPTER 2

"You got your toothpaste?"

The question shook the memory from Lucas's head.

"Huh?" He turned to look at his grandma behind the wheel. For days after the soldiers came, he'd often found her sitting on the porch, just staring up into the green mountainside above the trailer. Lucas never saw her cry much, but her red eyes told him she did it plenty when she was off by herself. But now, two months later, the light had returned to those eyes, and she was back to poking fun at him when he deserved it.

"Toothpaste," she repeated. "If I know you, it's the one thing you forgot."

Lucas hated to admit she was right. "I'll just borrow some at the camp."

"Maybe there ain't any," his grandma joked. "It ain't exactly some fancy motel you're off to."

Lucas only shrugged. He didn't need to be reminded that his home for the next week was about to be a camp filled with a bunch of strangers, most of them rich city kids that probably wouldn't give two farts about him and his kind.

His grandma had gotten the invitation about a month before school let out. Camp Kawani. Some kind of summer camp up in the Blue Ridge Mountains of Virginia. A camp for kids like him. Or at least kids with a dead ma or pa. Somehow they'd known about his pa, about how he died, and just the thought that someone up here knew something like that about his life still gave him the jitters. After three days of hollering at his grandma and the school counselor who came all the way up into Indian Hole to tell him all the *wonderful* things she'd heard about Camp Kawani, he'd finally given up. But ever since they'd pulled onto the pavement that morning and headed east, the reality of spending a week away from everyone and everything he'd ever known had his stomach churning.

They'd followed the county road to Highway 16, alongside stretches of creeks turned black and rusty from being downstream of the sludge leftover from mountaintopping. Once, where they had a long-distance view, Lucas saw a ragged and massive slash of gray among the rolling blanket of green. Even from miles away, it looked like the surface of the moon brought down to Earth.

Almost three hours from Indian Hole, they finally crossed into Virginia not once but twice, following the narrow two-lane over ridge after ridge of hazy, blue-green mountains lined up like the waves of an ancient, frozen sea. At the western foot of the Blue Ridge, they crossed the James River into a town that was the busiest they'd seen the whole trip. The street was lined with neat, brick-fronted buildings that were a mix of businesses for the locals with a few art galleries and gift stores thrown in for the tourists.

"We oughta be able to find you some toothpaste here, don't you think?" his grandma said, eyeing the signs on the buildings. "Maybe a decent lunch too. Could be the last one you get for a week." Lucas didn't find the humor in that, but he also wasn't going to argue about eating in a restaurant, an experience he could probably number on two hands. His grandma spied a little market and found a space for the truck on the next block.

Lucas followed his grandma to the market and went in through a screen door tucked between crates of vegetables for sale on the sidewalk. A man standing behind the front counter greeted them. "Can I help you two find something?" he said.

"Toothpaste?" asked Lucas's grandma.

"Three aisles down, near the end." The clerk looked at Lucas. "You're headed up to that camp today, aren't you?

The question caught Lucas off guard. Did everybody in this part of Virginia know about him? Without meeting the clerk's eyes, he replied with a quick nod and headed off to find the toothpaste. The man spoke to Lucas's grandmother in a low voice that he could still hear from the back of the little store.

"Sorry. I just know Sunday's usually the first day up at Camp Kawani. Already had a couple kids about his age stopping in. Last-minute supplies, you know."

"Don't worry yourself," answered Lucas's grandmother quietly. "He's just a little nervous about bein' away from home. That and a lot of bad news lately."

Lucas returned quickly with a box of toothpaste. He had just reached the counter when a shadow crossed the window. The clerk turned toward the door with a smile, ready to greet his next customer. But just as suddenly, the smile vanished, and Lucas heard him whisper, "Oh, Lord..." under his breath.

The man who walked in was older than Lucas's grandmother, but he walked quickly, without a stoop, and his bright blue eyes gave him an electric kind of energy. His bare arms looked as if they were carved out of a knotty old tree, and the skin of his face and neck was baked into brown leather, like he'd spent a lifetime working hard in the sun. He wasn't big, but something about the way he walked or the cords of muscle in his arms made him seem much younger than the years on his face. His snow-white beard was untrimmed and stained with a streak of brown that looked like tobacco spit, and the knife and sheath on his belt looked like something out of the pioneer days.

The man brushed past him, and Lucas caught an odor of pipe smoke mixed with sweat. His grandmother tried to greet the man with a nod, but he ignored her.

The clerk spoke cautiously to him, "Afternoon, Mr. Creech," but the old man headed for the back of the market without replying.

Grimacing at Lucas's grandmother, the clerk threw up his hands. "Sorry," he whispered. "Most folks around here are a lot friendlier. Not that one."

The man rummaged around in the last aisle, cursing under his breath in a low, angry growl. When he came back to the counter, he carried a heavy sack of sugar, gripping it with the fingers of one hand as if it weighed nothing. The other hand clutched four pouches of pipe tobacco. He spoke to the clerk as if Lucas and his grandmother weren't even there.

"When you gonna get some real tobacco in here?" His growling voice sounded like two rough slabs of stone scraping together. "This stuff smokes like it came out the back end of a horse."

"Mr. Creech, sir," the clerk said timidly, "there's women and children here."

The old man glanced down at Lucas as if noticing him for the first time. "So there are. You think that boy don't hear a lot worse in school these days?" The clerk began to speak again, but the old man's eyes flashed angrily. "Just sell me these and don't be lecturin' me about my language."

He tossed the sack of sugar onto the counter with a solid thump. The tremor from the heavy bag knocked over a small stand of key chains, scattering a few of them onto the floor at the man's feet. Instinctively, Lucas bent down to help gather them up. But as he started to place them back on the stand, the old man snatched them out of his hand as quick as a striking snake.

"Do I look feeble, boy?" he snarled, glaring down at Lucas with his ice-blue eyes.

Lucas started to stammer something in response, but before he could, his grandmother spoke up sharply. "Sir, I don't know you from Adam, but I do know that ain't no way to treat a boy showin' good manners."

The man's eyes left Lucas, and he turned his wrath on Lucas's grandmother. "You're right about one thing, woman," he growled, "you *don't* know me from Adam. And I don't expect you want to."

Any other time, Lucas would have kept his mouth shut, especially with his grandma hovering near. But the stranger's harsh words for her bottled up with the idea of being stuck up in the camp for a week had him ready for a scrap. Even with a crazy old stranger. He caught the man's stare and gave it right back.

"Maybe you *are* feeble," he answered, "if that's how you talk to ladies and kids."

"Lucas!" his grandmother exclaimed, but her reaction didn't distract the old man. His fearsome eyes were back on Lucas now, and a wicked smile curled across his lips, as if he were already enjoying the thought of the whipping the boy had just invited on himself.

The look raised the hairs on Lucas's neck, but he wasn't about to apologize.

The old man put a hand on the butt of his knife. "You need a lesson in respectin' your elders, boy?"

But the clerk raised a trembling hand to calm him. "Now, Mr. Creech, the boy was just trying to be h…h…helpful," he stuttered. "You ask me, it's too bad there aren't more youngsters like that."

The old man met the clerk's eyes with a deadly glare, and his words came out like the long blade of a knife scraping slowly across a sharpening stone.

"You can take that hand out of my face," he snarled, unsnapping the sheath on his belt, "or you'll be learnin' to work that cash register with just one."

The clerk's hand dropped quickly, and the color drained from his face. Lucas's grandmother put her finger to his lips, signaling Lucas to keep quiet. By now, he didn't need the signal. It was obvious the old man was a dangerous mix of mean and crazy.

The old man's glare dropped to a stack of pamphlets piled in a box on the counter. The words "Beale Treasure Codes—50 cents" were scrawled on the front of the box. He picked one up and turned it over in his hand. Lucas noticed a crude drawing of a treasure chest, coins and jewels spilling out, on the front of the pamphlet.

"Still sellin' this sorry old story too," said the old man. He crumpled the pamphlet in his hand and bounced it off the clerk's chest. "I ever find one of those on someone up on my land, I'll come for *you* soon as I'm done with them."

The clerk rang up the man's purchase quickly, without another word. While he did, the old man kept his eyes on Lucas, letting him know the challenge wasn't forgotten.

When the screen door finally slammed behind the old man, the clerk let out a long breath and some of the color seeped back into his face. Lucas realized he'd been holding his own breath too.

Lucas's grandmother laughed nervously. "He always that angry?" she asked, motioning her grandson to pick up the fallen key chains now that the coast was clear.

"Well, insane's more like it, I hate to say. He lives way up Moccasin Hollow, all by his lonesome. Other side of the ridge from that camp you're going to, in fact. He's like some kind of leftover from the old days. Lives mostly on whatever he can kill. No phone, no car. Still uses an outhouse even." He scrunched up his face as if nothing could be more backward than an outdoor toilet, and Lucas couldn't help thinking about the old one they still used back in Indian Hole when the trailer's was occupied or busted.

"Fortunately he only comes down here every few months. Buys a few things from me, usually curses me out or threatens me in the process, and spends the rest of his time over in the library across the street. After that, he just walks back out of town, sometimes way after dark."

"Why doesn't someone just take him down a notch?" asked Lucas's grandmother.

"Well, what with his reputation and all, no one's willing to try. Folks say one time he caught a couple of treasure hunters digging up his orchard. Ol' Giddy—that's what folks call him around here—he claimed they swung a shovel on him. All I know is one ended up with both arms busted, and the other had to have a load of bird shot taken out of his behind. Sheriff took six deputies with him when they brought Ol' Giddy in for that one. Should've gone to jail for a spell, but the judge bought his self-defense story." He snickered. "Ol' Giddy was just lucky that particular judge hadn't been around long enough to know his reputation."

"Why were they diggin' on his land?" asked Lucas's grandmother. "The treasure hunters, I mean."

The clerk brightened, clearly relieved to change the subject. "Oh, I guess you haven't heard about our local legend? Supposed to be millions in gold and silver buried up in these mountains—or so the legend goes." He pointed to the stack of brochures on the counter. "Usually, I try to hide these when Ol' Giddy comes around. Didn't get the chance today." He took one of the pamphlets and handed it to Lucas. "Take it, son. It's the least I can do for you standing up to my ugliest customer."

Lucas held the brochure but didn't open it.

"There's some lists of numbers in there. They're codes. The first one's supposed to tell you where the treasure is. Of course, folks have been trying to figure 'em out for around a hundred fifty years, so good luck. Personally, I think the whole thing is just an old hoax, but it helps me sell a metal detector now and then."

They paid for the toothpaste and walked back down the block to the truck. Lucas tossed the treasure codes onto the seat next to him. He wasn't feeling all that lucky.

His grandmother noticed and dropped the pamphlet into the bag with the toothpaste. "Hey now," she said, glancing across the seat at him, "you might need that. Maybe you'll get a chance to do some treasure hunting up there at the camp."

She started up the truck and gazed out the windshield, the smile leaving her voice. "Sure could use some right about now, couldn't we?"

Lucas didn't answer. He just looked at the mountains looming ahead.

Sure could.

CHAPTER 3

Outside of town, the road narrowed, switchbacking its way up the west side of the Blue Ridge. Lucas caught glimpses between the trees, down to the farmland they had just crossed. The air rushing in through the truck's open windows was still humid, but up here it was a little cooler and smelled of rotting logs and evergreen needles. Every so often the roadside cliffs glistened with tiny cascades bubbling straight from the rock, like the mountains' cold blood seeping from veins opened by the slice of the highway.

They passed a sign telling them they had entered a national forest, and after that the only buildings in sight were the tin-roofed farmhouses far below. Once they reached the crest of the mountains, Lucas's grandmother asked him to read the directions to the camp aloud, and they finally spotted the tiny, moss-covered sign for Camp Kawani partly hidden by a tangle of roadside vegetation. The forgotten little marker made the camp seem even lonelier, like whoever ran it wanted it completely isolated from the outside world. When they turned onto the gravel road leading to the place he would spend the next seven nights, the knot in Lucas's stomach tightened.

Half a mile down the entrance road, they came out of the trees into a narrow, grassy valley surrounded by forested ridges. Lucas's grandmother slowed the truck in front of a small cabin with a stone foundation and a hand-lettered sign tacked to the front porch that read "Camp Kawani Check-In." Another vehicle, a pickup much newer than theirs, was stopped in the small parking area.

Lucas forced himself out of the car and surveyed the layout of the place as he followed his grandmother toward the office. The road they were on looped around two rows of four cabins that faced each other across a grassy space. At the far end of the cabins sat a log building with high, horizontal slits for windows, and doors at either end. Behind it were several stacks of brightly colored canoes and kayaks. A circle of log benches surrounded a blackened fire pit at the center of the lawn between the cabins, and a squat stone tower with a large, brass bell on top overlooked the fire circle. *Probably what they ring when a kid tries to escape*, Lucas imagined.

Beyond the buildings, a raised wooden platform perhaps ten feet high looked out over a long, blue-green lake that filled the rest of the valley floor. Though the water looked cold, a few kids were already swimming, and a couple more were doing cannonballs and jackknifes off the platform. The lifeguard, an older boy in a light blue T-shirt, watched from a chair at the top of the platform. Attached to a stout pole on his platform was one end of a long steel cable that swooped out over the lake and disappeared high in the trees on a hill at the far end.

Lucas's grandmother had stopped and was watching him. "Looks like fun, don't it?" she said.

"Looks like a bunch of city kids swimmin' in a pond for the first time in their life," Lucas grumbled.

She ignored his sour mood and stepped up onto the porch. A wooden plaque bolted above the door was inscribed with the camp's name and a quote from someone named John Muir. He paused to read it while his grandmother went into the office.

I am well again, I came to life in the cool winds and crystal waters of the mountains.

Whatever, thought Lucas.

Inside the office, a redheaded woman standing behind the front desk looked their way and smiled. Her hair was drawn back in a long ponytail, and her face was tanned and sprinkled with freckles. The woman wore the same light blue T-shirt as the lifeguard outside.

She was busy talking with a short, dark-skinned man and

a boy about Lucas's age. *Mexican or something*, Lucas figured. The boy might have been a little older than Lucas, and even though he was shorter, he looked solid enough. He wore a pair of basketball shoes, and the green backpack leaning against his leg looked new. Unlike Lucas's buzz-cut dirty-blond hair, the boy's was longer, nearly in his eyes, and shiny black like a chunk of raw coal.

The woman behind the desk gave the father and son directions to a cabin, telling them they could pull up behind it to unload. As the boy hoisted the pack onto one shoulder and turned to head out the door, he caught Lucas's eye and gave him a quick, nervous nod. The look on the boy's face reminded Lucas of the feeling in his own stomach.

Lucas's grandmother stepped up to the counter to introduce herself, and the woman at the desk shook her hand.

"Welcome to Camp Kawani," she said, smiling. "Hope you didn't have any trouble finding us. I'm Maggie Cates." Then, without glancing at the list of names on the counter, she turned to Lucas and stuck out her hand. "I'm guessing you are…Lucas, right?"

Lucas remained silent but shook her hand. He recognized her name as the one on his invitation. Outside, he heard the pickup's doors creak open and slam shut and the sound of crunching gravel as the truck headed toward the cabins.

"Let's get you checked in," Maggie said, looking him over.

She spent a minute going over some forms with Lucas's grandmother, then spoke to Lucas as his grandmother signed them. "Did you check the place out before you came in?"

"Sort of," Lucas replied.

"Good. I guess you noticed we have two rows of cabins. Boys are on the left, girls on the right. That big building down at the end is the bathhouse, with bathrooms and showers." She grinned. "Don't worry, it's modern, not like an outhouse or anything, but you still have to walk to get to it."

"Sure," Lucas muttered, not bothering to tell her he had outhouse experience.

"If you need to make a call home, you'll have to make it from the office here. I don't know if you have a cell phone with you, but we don't have coverage down in this valley, and even out by the road, it's pretty spotty."

Lucas nodded. He'd never had his own phone, but he didn't plan on calling home anyway.

"Our dining hall is up in the woods past the lake." She pointed to a map of the camp on the wall behind the desk. "If we're not out on the trail somewhere, that's where we eat all our meals. The recreation barn next to it has a climbing wall, ping-pong and pool tables, and some other good stuff."

Lucas was only half listening. Outside he heard a small engine start up. A man on a mud-covered, yellow-and-black four-wheeler motored past the window behind Maggie and turned up the road into the cabins. He was towing a small trailer loaded with boxes and cans. The driver gunned the engine loudly, like he was about to accelerate, and looked over his shoulder at the office window. Easing off the throttle, he shot a wave back at Maggie through the blue smoke of the four-wheeler's exhaust.

Maggie waved back and shook her head. "My brother, Aaron. You'll meet him later. That four-wheeler's his favorite toy. That's probably part of your dinner it's hauling up the hill right now."

"Do we get to ride it?" asked Lucas, though he already figured the four-wheeler was off-limits. He'd never had one of his own, but back when he'd lived with his pa—and closer to his friends—he'd gotten to ride one a few times.

"You're not the first to ask," she replied. "Actually, we like to stick to *non*-motorized activities around here. Still fun, I promise, just quieter. Did you see our zip line? No one's died on it...yet," she said smiling. "You'll get to try it this afternoon. We find that screaming for your life is a good way for the other campers to get to know you."

They heard the gravel crunching again as the other pickup rumbled past the office and back toward the highway. Maggie turned back to Lucas's grandmother. "Looks like you're just about finished up with the paperwork. Cabin One is the first one down the left fork."

Lucas and his grandmother piled back into the car and

pulled up behind Cabin One. A set of steps led up to a landing and a screen door. Once he went through that door, the only faces Lucas would see for a week would belong to strangers. The thought of not seeing his home for so long suddenly hit him hard, and he wished he'd put up more of a fight about the camp.

His grandma seemed to sense how he felt. "Lucas, I know this ain't where you want to be. Especially with all this bad news. But I think it's what your pa would want—to come up here and be with some other boys and girls goin' through what you're goin' through. Heck"—she nodded out the windshield at the lake and the green ridges surrounding the camp—"seems like an awful nice spot to clear your head, if you ask me."

Lucas didn't plan on clearing his head. "You expect me to just forget about Pa?"

"Lucas, you know that ain't what I mean. I know you'll never forget your pa. In fact, I got somethin' to help you with that while you're up here." She opened her door and went around to the bed of the truck. Lucas followed.

She pointed to the duffel bag he'd packed with a week's worth of clothes and gear for the camp. "You best lift that up. I surely can't."

Lucas hefted the duffel out of the truck. What she'd brought had been hidden underneath it all the way from

21

Indian Hole.

"They said you'd need one up here for the hiking they got planned for you," she said.

It was a Marine rucksack. Desert camouflage. WHITLATCH was stenciled in black across the back, right above the letters US.

His father's pack. The sight of it made him want to bawl like a baby.

"Dang, Grandma," he said, his voice breaking a little. "I can't take this. What if somethin' happens to it?"

"Lucas, that pack's already been through a lot worse." She looked around at the camp. "This here will be like a vacation for it."

Lucas shook his head, but he tossed the pack on top of the duffel at the foot of the cabin steps.

"Want me to go in with you? Help you get settled?" his grandmother asked.

Knowing his roommates could already be inside, Lucas figured he'd better keep the good-bye outside. "That's okay."

"All right then. But remember what I told you in the car. You have any trouble, you have them camp people call."

He knew she was having a hard time saying good-bye too. Lucas finally met her eyes. "I'll be fine."

"Then I'll see you next Saturday." His grandma started to get back in the truck but stopped. "Lucas, you need to remember these other young 'uns all had a rough spell, just like you. Some maybe rougher. Be good to 'em."

Lucas couldn't imagine anything rougher than the last two months of his life, but he nodded anyway. He watched her start up the truck and put it into gear. She made her way slowly around the loop road behind the girls' cabins and back toward the office. The old pickup finally disappeared beyond the trees, and the crunch of gravel faded, replaced by the shrieks and splashes of the campers at the lake.

Lucas hoisted his duffel onto one shoulder and picked up his father's pack, lugging them up the few steps to the screen door. He propped the pack against a railing and pulled open the door to the little cabin that would be his home for the next week. Inside, the first thing he saw was a new green pack.

The Mexican kid's from the office.

CHAPTER 4

Lucas stepped in quietly, catching the screen door so it wouldn't slam. The cabin was larger than it looked from outside. Besides two sets of bunk beds, the single room had a wall with built-in drawers and an open closet with hooks for hanging clothes and gear. The boy from the office wasn't inside, but his pack was tossed onto one of the bottom bunks, so Lucas hefted his bag onto the other one, across the cabin from the kid's.

Another screen door faced out to the front porch, and Lucas saw the kid out there. For a second, Lucas considered slipping out the back door and walking down to the lake or hiking up the hill to try and find the recreation barn. But the lake was swarming with other kids, and the barn probably would be too. He wished his grandma hadn't just reminded him to be friendly. He pushed open the screen door and stepped onto the front porch.

The boy was in the last of four plastic chairs, his bare feet up on the rail and his socks tossed next to him. He looked up when Lucas came out the door and shot him a quick, tight-lipped smile. Lucas nodded and said, "Hey," but the boy went back to staring straight ahead.

Lucas took the farthest chair from the boy and put his own feet up on the rail, trying to act just as relaxed. He remembered the boy's father's accent in the camp office and wondered if the roommate he was about to spend a week with even spoke English.

Three girls were on the front porch of the cabin straight across, chatting away as if they'd been friends all their lives. Their easy conversation only amplified the uncomfortable silence between the two strangers on the porch of Cabin One. After a long minute, Lucas finally spoke again.

"I hope they ain't plannin' on cacklin' like that all week," he said, lifting his chin toward the girls across the lawn.

The brown-skinned boy huffed out a laugh but didn't speak.

Lucas had had enough of the silence. "You speak English?"

The boy threw his head back and laughed out loud this time. "*Sí, mejor que tú!*"

Lucas was confused—and getting annoyed quick by the kid's squirrelly behavior. "So speak it then."

The boy laughed again. "I said, 'Yeah, I speak it better

than you.' I mean, sorry, I've just never heard someone talk like that. Except on TV, I guess. But I guess I've never been this far out of the city till today."

Lucas could have said the same about the boy's city accent, but instead he said, "Sorry. I guess I should've figured you could speak English. I just figured since you were just sittin' there not sayin' much. And you're a…"

This time the boy turned and faced Lucas. "I'm a what?"

Lucas wasn't sure how to say it, but he spit it out anyway. "A Mexican, right?"

"Seriously? A Mexican? Not even close," the boy said. "My dad's Salvadoran. You know, from *El Salvador*? It's a *country*. But, dude, I'm as American as you." He turned back in his chair, shaking his head as if Lucas were the dullest kid he'd ever met.

"Like I said, sorry," Lucas stammered. Meeting his first cabinmate wasn't exactly going well, and he had two more to go.

The boy shrugged but didn't look up, and within a few seconds, the silence had closed in on the porch again. It felt like the girls across the grass were sitting right there with them, ready to bust out laughing at whatever stupid words came out of Lucas's mouth. Other than being stuck at the same lousy camp, it looked like he had only one thing in common with the brown-skinned kid, and he sure wasn't going to start talking about their dead parents.

As if the kid read his mind, he leaned forward in his chair and propped his elbows on the railing of the porch. He stared across the lawn, but his mind wasn't on the noisy girls.

"We both know why we're here, right?" he said. "But that doesn't mean we've got to talk about it. Right?"

Lucas laughed nervously. "Hey, me neither. Don't even care." But he thought about how that sounded. *I don't care if your ma just died. Or my pa.* "I mean I don't care if we *talk* about it," he spit out.

The boy nodded, like he was okay with their agreement. He leaned back in his chair and let out a long breath. When he looked over at Lucas again, his fierce demeanor had vanished. "My name's Alex."

"Lucas. Lucas Whitlatch." Before he could say more, another car pulled to a stop behind one of the cabins closer to the lake. A girl and her mother got out, hauling out a blue pack and a rolled-up sleeping bag. They set the gear next to their car, and the girl's mother gave her a long hug. Then the girl picked up the gear and disappeared toward the back door of her cabin.

"Where you from, Lucas Whitlatch?"

"West Virginia," Lucas replied, aiming his thumb west. "Probably what you'd call the middle of nowhere."

"Actually, I thought *this* was the middle of nowhere. But then, I'm from DC. My backyard's about the size of this cabin." He looked around at the mountains. "All this nature and stuff kinda feels like another planet."

"Funny," Lucas said, "my backyard's pretty big." He could've told Alex plenty about the mountain, but he doubted a city kid could appreciate it much. Besides, he had a million questions to ask Alex about Washington. A couple of his friends had been, but he couldn't see his grandparents ever taking him, even if they could afford to.

He had just opened his mouth to ask when a loud crash from inside their cabin rattled the little building.

Lucas was through the door first. Another boy lay belly up at the foot of the ladder to the bunk above his. An enormous pack was strapped to his back, and he was rocking back and forth, struggling to get to his feet like an overturned turtle. Some of the pack's contents were scattered on the floor next to him, including a roll of toilet paper that had popped loose and rolled across the cabin floor, unfurling as it went.

The boy stopped moving and grinned sheepishly at Lucas and Alex as they came through the door. He stuck out his arms toward them.

"Little help here?" he said.

CHAPTER 5

Lucas and Alex had to use both hands to pull their room-mate to his feet. Though much shorter and a little younger, he was a lot rounder. His hair was red, and his cheeks were sweaty and pink from the struggle to get back on his feet. He wore clunky hiking boots and thick socks, and a green-and-gold T-shirt with the face of a bear surrounded by the name of a middle school. A big watch bristling with buttons was strapped to his wrist.

"Dude," asked Alex, "what happened?"

"I was trying to get my pack up there," the boy said, pointing to the top bunk.

Lucas reached for the boy's pack. "Why not just lift it… Dang! What's in this thing?" The pack felt like it was loaded with concrete.

"You know, gear and stuff. Maybe just a few snacks."

"And your personal toilet paper?" said Alex, handing the

roll back to the new kid.

The boy snatched the roll out of Alex's hand. "Hey, you ever seen the toilet paper in these places?" he asked. "It's like sandpaper. I went to a summer camp a couple years ago. You think the poison ivy and the bees and the rain are bad? I swear, the toilet paper in these places will give you a diaper rash so bad, it's like you've been eating Mexican food for a..."

The new kid stopped and studied Alex. "I mean, no offense."

"He ain't Mexican. He's Salva...salva-somethin'." Lucas chimed in.

"American." Alex shot Lucas a hard look. "Jeez."

"Yeah, American. That's what I meant."

"Sure." Alex rolled his eyes. "What's your name?" he asked the new kid.

"George. Funderburk," he replied.

"I'm Alex Cruz. This is Lucas Whitlatch."

"Cruz and Whiplash?" laughed George. "Sounds like some kind of cop show or something. Me, I usually get 'Thunderbutt' or 'Thunderburp' or something, but Cruz and Whiplash, that's pretty cool."

"Naw, it's Whit—*latch*. Like on a gate," said Lucas. "Hey, how'd you even get here? How come we didn't hear no car drive up?"

"My dad's idea," replied George. "He dropped me off at the office. Said I could get in some practice with the pack if I hauled it from there. Plus he's got a flight to catch tonight." His smile faded. "That's pretty much all he does—catch flights. Especially since my mom died."

Lucas and Alex stared at the floor, and the cabin went deathly silent, as if a shadowy hand had reached in and snatched away the easiness the three boys had just begun to feel.

"Jeez, what did I say?" asked George. "I mean, it's why we're here, isn't it?"

Lucas looked past George out the window. There were now four girls gathered on the porch across the lawn, looking like best friends already. "Yeah, but we ain't got to talk about it, do we?" he finally said.

George threw up his hands. "Hey, it's not like I'm planning on sitting around holding hands and crying all week. Look, I just want to go for a swim. That lake's probably cold as a penguin's butt, and I'm sweatin' like an Eskimo in Africa."

Lucas shook his head. "That how you always talk?"

"I was going to ask you the same thing," George said.

Alex laughed. "Guess we're going swimming," he said, unzipping his pack.

A few minutes later, Alex and George had changed into swimsuits, but Lucas still had on his shorts. Back home, they worked for swimming in the creek too.

They were heading for the front door when they heard

the crunch of gravel and the idling of an engine behind their cabin. Through the back door, Lucas could make out enough of the car to tell it was a big, expensive sedan. A door opened, and they heard a man's voice.

"Please remain in the car while I retrieve your bags, Zachary."

George looked at the other two boys and mouthed the words, *Retrieve your bags?* He arched his eyebrows and gave a comical bow toward the door.

A pale, stiff-looking man struggled into the cabin lugging an expensive-looking backpack and an overstuffed duffel bag. He wore a crisp, white shirt and red tie, with perfectly creased dark pants. He looked completely out of place in the rustic cabin, and his uncomfortable expression let them know he wasn't thrilled to be in such uncivilized surroundings. Without acknowledging them, he dropped the pack and bag next to the open closet and scurried back out the screen door. His exit was followed shortly by a boy's voice.

"Tell my father I made it here alive. And don't be surprised if he calls you to pick me up early. I doubt I can take a week in this dump."

The boy who came through the screen door looked perhaps a year older than them. Lucas wasn't skinny—"lean" is what his grandma called him all the time—but this kid was big in the chest and shoulders, like some of the eighth grade kids who played football at Lucas's school. He wore a backward, flat-brimmed cap, with bright blond hair poking out from under it. Slung over one shoulder was a slick, brightly colored daypack with a rubber water tube hanging out of the top. Like his clothes, the pack looked straight off the store shelves. And expensive.

George was the first to speak. "Welcome to Camp Misery," he said with a goofy grin.

The new boy ignored him. Instead, he unzipped one of the pockets of his pack, retrieved a metallic red smartphone and plugged a set of earbuds into it. He tossed the phone and the pack up onto the bunk George had just tried to claim.

"I guess this one's mine, huh," he said and started to climb up the ladder.

Lucas spoke up. "Actually, George was…"

The older boy froze, one foot on the ladder, and stared over his shoulder at Lucas.

"George was what?" he asked, more annoyed than threatening. But it was hard not to be intimidated by the older, bigger kid.

"He was going to take that one, but he didn't get a chance yet," replied Alex.

The kid grinned, enjoying the little confrontation. He continued up the ladder and plopped onto the mattress. He dangled his feet off the edge and made a show of looking around, even checking under the pillow. Then, raising his eyebrows in mock surprise, he looked straight at Lucas and said, "I don't see his stuff up here anywhere. Or his name."

Lucas looked back hard at the boy, but George, red in the face again, interrupted.

"Jeez, girls. Relax. No need to fight over me. One bunk's as good as the others."

Before Lucas could say anything else, the older boy said, "Great!" He lay back on his pillow, stuck his earbuds in, and began messing with his phone.

"Wasn't *we* goin' for a swim?" Lucas said, loud enough for the new kid to hear.

Alex threw his towel over his shoulder. "Yeah, I think *we* were."

A hand came off the phone and gave them a sarcastic, finger-wagging wave.

Outside, George said, "Is it me, or is that kid a total butthead?"

All Lucas could think about was his grandma and her pickup, already halfway back to Indian Hole.

CHAPTER 6

George Funderburk wasn't much of a swimmer, but his dives were another story. Standing atop the platform, pale belly jiggling, he would announce himself as the "Fabulous Flying Funderburk" and give a special name—like the "Lake Shaker" or the "Fish Flattener"—to each thunderous cannonball or jackknife he was about to perform. The one he simply called his "Thunder Butt," a cannonball requiring a two-handful grab of his rear end, quickly became the crowd favorite, at least for some of the other boys. The girls, on the other hand, either shook their heads in embarrassment or tried to ignore George and his enormous splashes. When the camp bell sounded, Lucas had nearly forgotten their surly roommate back in Cabin One.

Maggie's voice came over the loudspeaker. "Attention, all campers, please meet at the top of the zip line. Bring your swimsuits and your courage. No wimping out allowed."

The swimmers cheered and began swimming to shore. As Lucas, Alex, and George dried off, they saw other kids emerging from their cabins. Just when they thought their roommate wouldn't take part, they saw him bound off the porch of Cabin One, a towel draped from his shoulders and white, wraparound sunglasses pushed back on top of his long, blond hair.

"At least he's not planning on playing with his phone all week," muttered George.

"Yeah, and if we hurry, he'll still be stuck at the back of the line when we're already flying across the lake," said Alex.

The three boys hustled up the hill, following the campers and the counselor ahead of them into the forest above the head of the lake. When they reached the platform at the uphill end of the zip line, a counselor on top was already preparing the first rider. From the base of the platform, where the line was beginning to form, they could see the zip line's entire route through the trees, out over the lake, and all the way down to the far end near the bathhouse. At the end of the long downhill flight, two other counselors in blue camp shirts waited to receive the riders.

They watched as the first rider, an older girl, was strapped into the harness dangling from the cable. The counselor gave her some last-minute instructions, then, with a gentle shove, sent her zipping down through the trees and out over the water. Hoots and cheers erupted from the waiting campers when the girl plunged off the platform and hurtled downhill, screaming the entire way. After what seemed like a full minute of zipping high across the water, the girl came to a gentle, gliding stop into the arms of the two counselors at the other end.

George was in front of the other two boys. "This is going to be awesome!" he declared.

"Yeah, if you don't poop your pants on the way down, George," joked Alex.

"Are you crazy?" he replied, smacking his hands on his freckled, white belly and grabbing a couple handfuls of flab. "This body was meant for flying!"

Two girls in line behind them shuddered visibly. One, a skinny girl with frizzy red hair, whispered to her friend, "Did you see him? That was disgusting!"

George noticed the attention. "Pardon me, ladies, but once you've seen the Fabulous Flying Funderburk, you'll understand the meaning of aerodynamics." He struck a bodybuilder's pose, the strain of which caused him to accidentally emit a noisy fart.

The kids around them erupted in laughter, and the red-haired girl's friend said, "O...M...G!"

Lucas turned away, embarrassed, while Alex simply buried his face in his hands, trying not to laugh. "Jeez, George!" he exclaimed through his fingers.

"What?" he said, grinning proudly. "That's my jet power."

Just then they heard a loud voice in the line behind them. "Relax, people. I'm just catching up to my roomies." The blond-haired boy from their cabin was moving up through the line, leaving annoyed campers in his wake. When he reached the two girls behind them, he said, "Excuse me, ladies, but do you mind if I cut in front? These are my roommates."

The girl with the red hair pointed at George and said, "No problem. We're too close to that one's jet power anyway." George only struck another ridiculous muscleman pose for them.

The rich kid stepped up behind his three roommates and greeted them like best friends. "Hey guys, thanks for saving me a spot."

"You ain't takin' mine," Lucas replied, turning his back on the older kid.

"Whoa, take it easy, country boy," their roommate said, putting up his hands and pretending to be scared. "As long as I'm not back with the riffraff, right here's fine with me."

"Look," said Alex, "if you're gonna pretend we're your best buddies, maybe you can at least call us by our names. His is Lucas."

"Hey, no problem. Lucas it is. Mine's Zack. You girls ever ride a zip line before?"

No one replied, so Zack went on.

"So I figured. Me, I'm a total beast on these things. Did one in Costa Rica, another one up near Seattle, and, oh yeah, a *really* extreme one over in the Alps." He leaned forward and whispered smugly to Lucas, "Those are in Europe, in case you're wondering."

Another rider, a boy in bright green trunks, took a running jump and plummeted toward the lake. He threw his arms out to imitate an airplane, relying totally on the safety harness to keep him in the air. The crowd cheered again, some more nervously than others.

On top of the platform, the counselor in charge hollered down to the boys, "All right, guys, you four can climb up and get your flight instructions."

Zack muttered, "Lame," under his breath.

Lucas turned to face Zack. "So why run up here and cut in line if it's gonna be so lame?"

Before Zack could answer, the counselor got their attention. "Let's go, guys! We've got others waiting."

The four of them climbed the ladder and stood on the platform while the counselor launched into his instructions.

"Okay, guys, listen up." He had one hand on a black nylon harness for the rider's waist and thighs. It hung from a T-shaped metal bar attached to two wheels that rode on the cable above them. "It's pretty simple. Once I strap you in to the harness and give you the go-ahead, you get a running start and take off. You don't have to hold on to the T-bar if you don't want to, but I'd recommend it if you're a little scared. If you're *more* than a little scared, feel free to scream." He winked and lowered his voice. "It scares the other kids waiting in line."

"George here's gonna be screaming like a baby the whole way down," Zack taunted.

"Yeah? Watch me," replied George.

"Enough of that—listen up," said the counselor. "The most important thing to remember is this." He pointed to a brightly colored ring attached to a pin that went through two metal pieces at the top of the harness. "Read my lips, boys. *Do not pull—or even touch—the orange ring!* It's for the counselor on the other end to get you loose quickly. If it's pulled while you're zipping, you'll only be hanging on by your arms. You let go of the bar, you fall. You fall, you get hurt—probably bad. So keep your hands off the ring. Am I clear?"

Alex and George nodded and Lucas said, "Yessir." Zack just grinned, but since he appeared to be paying attention, the counselor didn't wait. "All right now. Who's up first?" he said.

George stepped up quickly and saluted the counselor, sucking in his gut and puffing out his chest. "The Fabulous Flying Funderburk, sir. Strap me in."

"Hey, Zack," said George, "you want extreme? Watch and learn."

"Yeah, watch out for his *extreme* jet power!" a girl at the foot of the platform yelled.

"All right," said the counselor, trying not to laugh. "The Fabulous, Jet-Powered Flying Funderburk it is."

It took him a little longer to strap George in because the thigh straps had to be loosened twice. When he was set, the counselor gave him the thumbs-up. Now attached to the line, George backed up past the other boys to get a running start. He paused to look down over the rail at the redheaded girl and winked at her. "This one's for you," he said.

The girl made a gagging sound and pretended to throw up, and Lucas and Alex buried their faces in embarrassment again. Then, like an overloaded bus with wings, George threw his arms straight out to his sides and began his takeoff roll for the edge of the platform.

At that moment, Zack made his move.

In one motion, he grabbed the orange safety ring above George's head and yanked it free. George saw what was happening but a second too late. He shot his hands up to the T-bar and tried to skid to a stop at the edge of the platform, but his momentum carried him off the edge. Immediately the cable sagged under his full body weight, bouncing him wildly up and down as he picked up speed through the trees.

Zack turned back to face Lucas and Alex. He was twirling the orange ring around his finger and beaming from behind his mirrored sunglasses. "There goes the Fabulous Flying Thunderbutt," he jeered. "Definitely extreme now."

The counselor took Zack by the arm.

"Take a seat on the bench!" he snapped, fumbling for the radio at his belt. "Get ready to go after this kid in the water!" he yelled into the radio at the lifeguards below. "A kid up here on the platform pulled the safety ring, and there's no way the one coming down is going to hold on!"

Most of the campers in line saw George's awkward takeoff, but only a few had seen Zack pull the ring. By the time the news raced through the crowd, George had hurtled out of the forest and over the lake, his body hanging like deadweight and his head pressed firmly between his pudgy arms as he strained to hang on. The campers grew quiet as the reality of George's predicament sunk in. Clear of the trees, he still had nearly a quarter mile to cross the lake. If he didn't hang on, he would tumble into the water from at least forty feet up. At high speed too.

"Hang on, George!" Alex yelled, but his words were lost in the ominous whine of the cable.

George, however, had no intention of crash landing.

Just when he reached the deepest part of the lake, the crowd on the hill heard a distant cry.

"THUUUNDER…BUUUTT!!!"

Lucas and Alex both whispered, "Oh no," as George's body dropped from the cable in a high-velocity plunge toward the lake.

Free from the T-bar, he brought his knees tightly to his chest and filled each hand with a generous fistful of rear end. With the precision of an Olympic diver going for the gold medal, he tucked his head and aimed his butt at the surface. Still bellowing when he hit the water, he executed a perfect entry, capping the cannonball with an enormous splash that echoed across the valley like an artillery blast.

By the time he surfaced and waved back at them, the other campers were cheering madly and howling with laughter. Lucas saw the smile drop from Zack's face.

The counselor was speaking angrily to someone on the radio, so he didn't notice Lucas and Alex leaping from the platform. They ran past the line of campers down to the lake edge and dove into the water. Lucas reached George first, just ahead of the lifeguard from the lake platform.

Swimming up, they saw that the younger boy was treading water and laughing loudly. Satisfied that George wasn't injured, the lifeguard gave a quick thumbs-up to the counselors at both ends of the zip line and turned to swim back to shore.

"So how'd it look, fellas? Nice entry? Good splash?" George asked.

CHAPTER 7

"You have…*got*…to be crazy," Alex replied in disbelief, gasping for air from the panicky swim out to George.

"Don't worry," Lucas snapped between breaths. "Zack ain't gettin' away with it."

"Hey, Lucas, come off it," Alex replied. "The counselors are pissed enough. They'll take care of him."

"Aww, who cares, you guys?" said George. "It was good entertainment, wasn't it?" Despite treading furiously, he started to sink a little lower. "Look, can we get outta here before I drown?"

They swam back to the edge of the lake and hauled themselves out. When they were up on the bank, George pointed up to the zip line platform in the trees.

"You guys are gonna miss your turn if you don't hurry back."

"What about you?" Alex asked. "You deserve another turn too."

"No, I'm good. Anything after that ride will just be a let-down for my fans. You guys go on back. I'm gonna go dry off."

He turned to walk along the lake back to their cabin. Alex started to walk back up to the woods, but Lucas didn't follow right away. He was still watching George lope toward the cabins.

"You coming?" Alex asked.

Lucas turned to follow Alex, shaking his head as he caught up. "He's mad," he said through gritted teeth. "He just won't let anybody see it."

"Yeah. So?"

"*So*, I don't know about you, but I seen enough trouble lately. I don't need no rich kid handin' me even more."

"Yeah. I know. It stinks. Maybe they'll put Zack in another cabin."

Just as Lucas and Alex began walking back up the hill, they saw Maggie and Aaron emerge from the trees. They were leading Zack in the opposite direction, toward the cabins and office. When Lucas drew close enough to see the cocky grin Zack was wearing, his anger boiled over.

Before Maggie could ask them if George was okay, he charged toward Zack and planted both hands hard on his chest, cursing him as he did. Zack staggered backward a few steps, but the bigger kid didn't go down like Lucas had hoped.

Aaron immediately restrained Lucas in a bear hug, not noticing Zack coming back at them.

With Lucas's arms pinned at his sides, Zack swung a right that caught him flush on the temple, a blow that flashed stars inside Lucas's head.

In a split second, Alex was rushing Zack, but Maggie stepped between them, her hands keeping them apart.

"ENOUGH!" she shouted angrily.

Zack ignored her and growled at Lucas. "Bring it, redneck."

"I will!" Lucas shouted back. But his left ear was ringing, and he was still wrapped in Aaron's arms.

"Maybe we'll *both* bring it," snapped Alex over Maggie's shoulder.

"Works for me," Zack replied with a smirk.

Maggie gave them both a hard shove in the chest. "I said ENOUGH!" She turned to her brother. "Let go of Lucas."

Aaron released his grip on Lucas but positioned himself so that Lucas couldn't get to Zack. Lucas wanted to rub the side his head, but he wasn't going to give Zack the satisfaction of knowing the punch had hurt. Bad.

"Lucas and Alex!" Maggie shouted. "Get up the hill! Aaron, you have a little talk with them on the way up." She put a hand on Zack's shoulder and herded him toward the office, but Zack shook loose of her grasp and faced Lucas.

"Maybe we'll have a little talk later too," he said, still smirking.

This time Aaron stepped threateningly toward the bigger

boy and pointed toward the office. "Go," he growled.

Zack pretended to shake in fear, as much at Aaron as at the other boys, but he turned to go with Maggie.

Aaron put his hands on Lucas and Alex and led them toward the zip line.

"So what was that crap all about?" Aaron asked, not trying to hide his anger.

"Zack coulda killed George!" replied Lucas. "And he thought the whole thing was a joke."

"And that's for us to handle, not you," said Aaron. "Right?"

"*Are* you going to handle it?" asked Lucas sarcastically.

"Yes," Aaron snapped back. "*We* will. Do you think this is the first time we've had a camper acting recklessly?"

"Well, I'm not rooming with him," said Alex. "That's for sure."

"No, you're not," said Aaron, "not after that. We keep a cabin empty just for situations like this. That's where he'll be tonight. Maybe for the rest of the week."

"So he gets a cabin to himself?" said Lucas, shaking his head. "Probably exactly what he had in mind."

"Do you have a better solution, Lucas?" said Aaron.

"Sure," interrupted Alex. "Just send him home."

"Well," said Aaron, "I'm sure that's what Maggie will be talking to him about in the office, right after they call his father to discuss the whole thing."

Lucas wanted to tell Aaron that was exactly what Zack

probably wanted too—to just go home. The bigger kid was probably using the counselors, and they didn't even know it.

They stopped at the back of the group of campers lined up for the zip line.

"You two try to have some fun today," said Aaron. "And don't even think about keeping this going with Zack. Any more fighting, and Zack won't be the only one we may have to send home early." He finally cracked a smile, trying to lighten up. "Seriously, guys, I wouldn't even talk to him unless it's to kiss and make up."

Lucas looked at Alex. "That sure ain't going to happen," he grumbled.

CHAPTER 8

Lucas, Alex, and George managed to steer clear of Zack the rest of the day. The older boy showed up for dinner, seemingly fine after his time in the office with Maggie. In fact, after he sat down with some other boys closer to his age, he did a lot of smiling and laughing. Most likely, Lucas figured, about the scare he had given George.

Lucas had just about concluded that Zack wouldn't even be punished when, near the end of dinner, he saw Aaron walk over and whisper something in his ear. Zack slumped a little then got up and joined the workers in the kitchen who were already scrubbing pots and washing dishes. Lucas heard later that Zack had gotten kitchen duty for a couple days as punishment. He'd be rising early to help with breakfast and staying late after dinner to clean. To Lucas, it still wasn't much for risking George's life.

As the sun was setting, the whole camp gathered around

the fire ring where a fire was already blazing. The only time Lucas was forced to talk was when they went around the circle, introducing themselves. Some of the kids seemed to think everyone ought to know a lot more about them, but he kept his introduction short—"Lucas Whitlatch, from West Virginia." It wasn't worth telling them "Indian Hole," because no one but his kin and a few more knew where that was, and it wasn't near any other place they would know either. Mostly he was thankful no one had to talk about why they were all there in the first place. After the counselors were done telling them some more about the camp and the hike they were going to take the next day, he stayed close to Alex and George but didn't say much. George did enough talking for all three of them anyway.

The next morning, the campers met up at the fire ring again before the hike. Lucas filled a water bottle at the sink in the bathhouse and threw an apple into his daypack before hurrying out to join the rest of the group. So far he had avoided running into Zack alone since the incident on the zip line.

All three counselors leading the hike that morning wore their blue Camp Kawani T-shirts and carried hefty daypacks with water bottles stuffed in both sides. Two of them looked like college kids—a wiry guy with a red beard and ponytail who introduced himself as Rooster and Sarah, a tall girl with a blue bandanna tying back her long, blond hair. Aaron was the leader.

A few campers grumbled when he reminded them that today's hike was only a "leg stretcher" for the longer, overnight trip they would start tomorrow, but he laughed off the complaints. "Hey," he said, motioning up at the ridgeline, "we've got twenty thousand acres here. And the best part is up there." He huddled with Rooster and Sarah for a minute before barking, "Okay, let's go," and setting off at a brisk pace up a trail into the woods.

The first part of the hike was all uphill, following a series of long switchbacks that worked their way up the side of the forested valley. Lucas was happy they'd started early. Even though the trail was mostly in the trees and the sun was just rising across the valley, the climb was hot and muggy.

Every once in a while, the hikers stopped at a rock outcrop or a break in the trees that opened up to views over the lake and cabins below. From up high, Lucas could see the layout of the entire camp, including the entry road leading out to the main highway. The sight of the way back home brought on a sudden rush of homesickness, and he spent the next half mile thinking how nice it would have been to be back in Indian Hole, eating his grandma's breakfast.

It wasn't long before the tough climb had separated the two dozen campers into three groups. In front were mostly older kids, including Zack, with Aaron keeping them from getting too far ahead. Most of the rest of the hikers were in the middle group, including some girls sticking close to Sarah and talking noisily as they walked. Lucas was in the last group with Alex, but not because they were slower than the other hikers. Instead, they hung back because George, red faced and soaked with sweat, was trudging up the side of the valley like he had a refrigerator on his back.

"Somebody...tell me...if we're almost...at the top," he wheezed. "I don't think...I can lift...my head."

"Dang, George, we ain't even come a mile yet," Lucas told him. For him, the hike was no different than the hundreds of times he'd been to the top of his own mountain.

Alex came up behind George and unzipped his pack. The younger boy was too exhausted to resist.

"Maybe I can take some of your load for you," he said. He looked into George's pack and found two full bottles of water, a melted and misshaped package of jumbo Snickers bars, along with the roll of George's personal toilet paper. He grabbed the roll and held it in front of George's face.

"Expecting an emergency, George?" he asked.

"I'm not...gonna...use a...pine cone," George huffed.

Lucas took the toilet paper from Alex and put it back in George's pack. Then he and Alex divvied up the rest of the items in George's pack to lighten his load.

"Thanks, guys…" George gasped. "I owe you."

After more uphill slogging, the slope began to ease, and the hikers crested the ridge. When Lucas cleared the trees, the view that opened up was as beautiful as any back home. At the top, the forest gave way to a broad meadow dotted with blue-gray boulders covered in splotches of bright green lichens. Ridge after ridge of blue mountains rolled off into the distance, each one a little lighter and hazier than the last. The only signs of people were the red and white dots of barns and houses in tiny pockets of pasture far below.

Out of the forest, the air was drier, and a breeze rustled the grass, cooling the sweat that had soaked Lucas's shirt. Aaron was right—it *was* way nicer up here, and it reminded Lucas of another rocky spot on their mountain back home.

A spot that would soon be gone forever.

Lucas had first caught wind of the plan for their mountain when he'd heard his grandfather on the phone not a month after the soldiers came. But it was more strangers driving up their road, this time in a shiny, mining company pickup that told him for sure. His grandpa had limped down to meet them. The men had unrolled a big map on the hood of the truck and talked over it for a long time, his grandpa doing a lot of pointing up at the ridges above the hollow. When the men shook his grandpa's hand one more time and headed into the woods and up the mountain, Lucas knew right then that the place more special to him than any other was going to die just like his pa.

He'd wanted to scream at them to stop. It even crossed his mind to find his pa's rifle. Instead, he just watched them disappear into the trees. Three hours later, he heard their truck start up and fade away down the road out of Indian Hole.

Lucas fought his grandparents about it as hard as a thirteen-year-old boy could. He told them they didn't need to sell, that if they could just hold out for a few more years, he could get a job when he turned sixteen. He reminded them that his pa, their son, had wanted the mountain protected, that it was one of his last wishes.

But his grandma had told him that his pa wanted Lucas protected even more, wanted them to have a future, and that the company's offer was enough to put them in a real house closer to town where it wouldn't be so hard to get him to school, with plenty left over to get his grandpa the doctoring he needed. In the end, there was nothing Lucas could do to stop it. A tiny, traitorous part of him even understood that selling the mountain was the only way his family, or what was left of it, would survive. But it wasn't the selling that was so bad—even his pa would have understood that they'd need the money with him gone. Instead it was the total destruction that made it so terrible.

He had seen that kind of destruction up close only once,

when he and his pa had hiked all day along the high ground connecting their mountain to Signal Ridge. After hours in the trees, surrounded by green, seeing the mountain top operation had felt so much like a punch in the gut that he was sure his knees had wobbled at that first sight of it.

They had looked straight down into an ash-gray valley that had once been as high as the ground where they stood. Giant yellow machines crawling across the pulverized landscape looked like insects next to scars cut two hundred feet high into the sides of the mountain. Bigger still were the terraces of leftover rock stacked in jarring, unnatural lines and looming over a poisonous lake the color of wood smoke and trapped against the foot of the barren mountain by a steep, gray dam. Lucas remembered thinking how impossible it seemed that something as small as a man, even hundreds of them with their machines, could do so much damage to something as big as a mountain.

And now, worst of all, he knew that this was his mountain's future too.

He and Alex sat down on a slab of rock and pulled out their water bottles while George made a big show of falling facedown in the grass. Without lifting his head, he reached out a sweaty arm and fumbled in his pack until he found a melted Snickers bar. Zack had found another rock, and Lucas was relieved to see he wasn't paying his ex-roommates any attention.

After the break, they wandered the ridgetop until mid-morning, resting for a final time on a huge flat rock that jutted out into thin air on one side. Sitting on the edge with a fresh breeze in his face and the dome of a cloudless sky all around him, Lucas felt like he was riding the nose of an airplane. He wished he could stay up high all day and not return to the gloom of the forest.

But Aaron wanted them back in camp for a late lunch, and soon they were walking downhill, along a trickle of water that grew into a noisy little creek lined with mossy boulders. Occasionally the trail crossed the water, but Lucas made no effort to keep his boots dry. At every crossing, he let the water soak through to cool his overheated feet.

George had just started dreaming out loud about how good the lake was going to feel when Aaron suddenly turned around and put both hands up to stop the caravan of hikers. After the shuffling of boots stopped and Rooster and Sarah had quieted the last talkers, the soft gurgle of the creek was the only noise in the forest. Lucas figured Aaron had seen an animal and was hushing everyone so it wouldn't run off.

But over the splashing water, he heard sounds that didn't belong deep in the forest. The metallic clink of a tool striking rock. And voices.

Aaron huddled with the counselors. After a few seconds, he and Rooster crept off through the woods while Sarah went down the line of campers, her finger to her lips.

"What's going on?" asked George. "Are they moonshiners?"

Sarah shook her head. "No, we don't have any moonshiners left around here," she whispered. "They're just trespassing on camp property, that's all."

"What's Aaron going to do to them?" asked a girl behind Lucas.

Before Sarah could answer, they heard shouting from back in the forest where the counselors had gone. It was Aaron. They could hear his angry words, but not what the trespassers were saying.

"No, you're on *private* property!…Sorry or not, I'll be calling the sheriff!"

One of the men said something Lucas couldn't make out, but Aaron's response was loud and clear.

"And you're wasting your time! We've got holes all over this county because of people like you, and not one of them ever had anything in it but dirt. Just go!"

The hikers heard the snapping of branches as Aaron and Rooster made their way back to the trail. Plowing angrily through the woods, Aaron looked at Sarah and said, "Just more treasure-hunting idiots. Let's get these kids back to camp." He stormed off down the trail, and the campers had to hurry to catch up.

"Treasure?" George raised his eyebrows.

"I heard somethin' about it yesterday," Lucas told the others. "Some guy in a store near here said it was millions in gold and silver. Had somethin' to do with secret codes. 'Course there's always treasure stories like that in these parts. Ain't none of 'em ever true."

"I don't know," replied Alex. "Those guys must have had *some* reason to hike all the way up here and dig a hole in the middle of nowhere."

They hadn't noticed Zack closing in behind them on the trail. But he'd been listening in on their conversation. Passing them, he looked Lucas straight in the eye.

"Stupid hillbillies," he said, grinning. "Probably so poor they'd do anything for money." He kept smiling and looking back, hoping for a reaction out of Lucas, but Lucas just let him pass. He wouldn't let Zack goad him into a fight. Not here at least.

A half mile later, Aaron finally slowed his angry pace. He began drifting back along the line of campers, letting them know that the encounter with the treasure hunters was nothing to worry about, and that he probably wouldn't even call the sheriff. Still, Lucas could tell Aaron was bothered by the trespassing strangers who had interrupted their hike.

"What were they looking for?" he asked tentatively when Aaron came up beside them.

"Oh, just an old legend. They won't find anything."

"How do you know?" asked Alex.

Aaron didn't answer at first. He stopped at a heavy tree branch that had fallen across the trail and waited for the rest of the group to negotiate their way over it. "You guys help me with this," he said, and the four of them lifted the branch to the side of the trail. Brushing the dirt from his hands, he turned to the boys.

"I tell you what," he said. "I think we'll answer everybody's treasure questions tonight."

CHAPTER 9

That evening, with the valley in deep shadow and the last of the sunset sky turning to twilight, the campers gathered around the central fire ring. While Maggie made sure the fire caught, Aaron went over the next day's plans. They would head off on a backpacking trip and spend two nights camping out.

"Our camp land is surrounded by a big roadless area on two sides," he explained. "The Preacher Rocks Wilderness. By hiking a loop through it, we can do a nice three-day trip."

Everyone there already knew the backpacking trip was on the week's schedule, but a few of the campers still groaned about lugging heavy packs and leaving their real beds behind.

Aaron ignored the complainers. "The rules of the wilderness area say we can't have more than fifteen in one group. So that means the girls will head out in one direction on the loop, and the boys will go the opposite way. Somewhere on the second day, we'll pass each other. And seeing as we're doing the trip in the middle of the week when everybody else is working, that'll probably be the only time we'll see anyone else."

A lot of the campers had questions, and by the time Aaron finished answering them, Maggie had the fire blazing. She sat down among the campers and spoke above their chatter.

"Listen up, everyone." She looked across the fire at her brother. "I understand you ran into some treasure hunters today, and Aaron says some of you have questions about our little treasure legend. So I guess that will have to be our story tonight."

"But," her brother chimed in, "if we tell this story, you all have to promise us one thing—nobody gets gold fever."

"What's that?" asked a lanky boy sitting next to Lucas.

"It means no one goes crazy and wanders off thinking they're going to find an imaginary treasure. You do that, and there's a way better chance you'll end up lost or hurt or dead."

"Are you kidding?" Zack piped up. "Maybe if you're totally desperate for money." He was just sitting down with the group, late from his kitchen duty. He aimed the comment across the fire at Lucas. For a second, Lucas caught his eye and glared back.

Aaron shot Zack a look too before addressing the group again. "So do we have a deal?"

The campers nodded and muttered in agreement.

But Aaron hesitated and looked up at the black ridges silhouetted against the twilight, like the mountains themselves might be listening. "You know, Maggie, we really aren't supposed to tell them about the treasure."

"Oh, come on, Aaron. Stop being so creepy about it. I'll tell it if you won't." She stared into the fire, searching for the right place to begin.

"So, there used to be a little crossroads town called Buford's down at the foot of these mountains. In the winter of 1820, a stranger named Thomas Jefferson Beale walked into the town's inn. The owner, a guy named Robert Morris, didn't know exactly where Beale was from, only he was a Virginian. He described him as tall and strong, with a dark tan, like he'd spent a lot of time somewhere in the sun. He also said Beale was a real lady's man."

"I can relate," interrupted George. A couple of the girls groaned.

Maggie continued. "Beale stayed at Morris's inn for the whole winter and left with some other men from Virginia in the spring, supposedly to hunt buffalo and grizzly bear out west on the Great Plains. Morris pretty much forgot about him. But two years later, Beale was back at the inn for another winter. By then, he'd learned of Morris's reputation as one of the most trustworthy men in this part of the state. So this time, Beale left something behind—a small, locked box—and he made Morris promise to keep it safe until he returned. And Morris did just what he promised. He locked the box away in a safe place and kept it a secret, even from his own family.

"Morris only heard from Beale one more time, in a letter from St. Louis two months later. Beale wrote that he was off again to hunt out west and that he wouldn't return for another two years. He told Morris that the box contained important papers and losing them would cost Beale and his men a lot of money. He also told Morris that the papers were written in code and that if he didn't return on schedule, a friend of Beale's would bring him the key, and Morris would be able to decipher them."

"So what happened?" asked a girl sitting next to Maggie. "Did he ever come back?"

"Nope," replied Maggie. "No one ever saw Beale or any of his men again. If the story is even true, they probably got lost in a blizzard or killed by Indians or something."

"So did the dude finally crack open the box?" Zack asked impatiently.

"Well," she said, "the friend with the key to the code never showed up like Beale promised. Finally, after waiting for years, Morris opened the box. What he found inside was a puzzle that tortured him for the rest of his life."

She poked at the fire with a long, charred stick, letting her words hang over the circle of campers for effect. Some of the kids finally urged her on and she continued.

"Three of the papers inside were the codes that Beale had described. Long sets of numbers. But each one had a title to tell what would be revealed if they were decoded—one gave directions to a secret vault in the Blue Ridge Mountains, the second described the treasure it held, and the third listed the names of Beale's men and where they lived in Virginia, so that the treasure could be given to their families if they never returned. In the other papers, Beale wrote the story of how he and his men had found gold and silver in a hidden canyon at the foot of the Rockies and mined it for close to four years. And how they'd made two separate trips back to Virginia to hide it in the mountains." She swept her hand across the skyline. "Supposedly, these mountains right here."

"Or so the story goes." Aaron stood up to throw another log on the fire. "Remember, you all, it's just a story."

"Sorry, Aaron," she replied. "Sometimes even I forget that. So anyway, now Morris was finally seeing what was inside Beale's secret box. The papers also told him that because he'd been trusted with the box and the treasure, Morris was also supposed to get an equal share."

"But everything was in code," said Alex.

"Right," she replied. "Without the key, he worked at it for years before he finally figured out one of the three ciphers—the one describing the treasure itself. The key for that one was the Declaration of Independence."

"Makes sense," said a girl next to Maggie. "Beale was named after Thomas Jefferson."

"Yeah, but how'd it work?" George asked.

"Pretty simple once you have the key. You start by numbering each word of the Declaration. Each of the numbers in the cipher match a word in the Declaration. So, say, the third number in the cipher is fifty-six, you look for the fifty-sixth word in the Declaration. If it started with a *J*, you plug a *J* into the cipher. Stick a bunch of letters together, you get words. When Morris did it with the second cipher, it spelled out what was in the treasure."

She stopped, working up the suspense until the campers were begging her to tell them what the cipher said.

"Oh," she answered, as if the treasure wasn't much, "only about two tons of gold and almost six tons of silver. Not to mention some jewels that Beale traded for on his way back to Virginia."

"Jeez! Two tons of gold!" shouted a boy across the fire from Lucas. But he looked puzzled. "How much would that be worth, anyway?"

"Duh, like, millions of bucks," jeered Zack.

"Actually, Zack, more like *a hundred* million today, and that's just the gold," said Maggie. "There's the silver and the jewels too. Anyway, the cipher said more." She took a folded sheet of paper from her back pocket and read. "'The above is securely packed in iron pots with iron covers. The vault is roughly lined with stones and the vessels rest on solid stone and are covered with others.'" She looked up at the campers. "And here's the most important part: 'Paper number one'—that's the first cipher—'describes the exact locality of the vault so that no difficulty will be had in finding it.'

"Supposedly not far from this camp. *Supposedly.*" She folded the paper and slipped it back in her pocket. "Morris died before he could figure out the other two codes, including the one that told where the treasure was hidden. He eventually sold them to a printer he knew, but the printer didn't have any better luck, so he printed up a little story about the treasure complete with the codes and sold it to anyone who was interested. That's why it's not a secret anymore."

"And *that's* why we have treasure hunters in our woods," added Aaron.

Maggie continued. "Yeah, ever since then, people have either been trying to break the other two codes or just hoping to find the treasure with a metal detector and some dumb luck. Some of world's best code breakers have even taken a crack at the codes. But even using supercomputers, no one's ever had any luck breaking them. Some think it's because the document Beale used for the other key is something really rare, just the opposite of something famous like the Declaration of Independence. Something small and simple. So rare that maybe there's only one copy in the whole world."

Maggie let the story sink in. Aaron got up again to tend the fire. As he did, Zack stood and began walking toward the bathhouse.

"Are you leaving us, Zack?" asked Maggie.

"Just need to go to the restroom, if that's okay," he said.

Lucas immediately wondered if the older boy was up to something. He glanced over at George and Alex, who had the same look of suspicion on their faces.

Aaron watched Zack walk toward the bathhouse before continuing the treasure story. "Of course," he said, "most people around here, including me, figure there's a simpler explanation. We figure the whole thing is a fancy hoax.

"The treasure hunters who come around with metal detectors usually only succeed in trespassing or getting lost. There are caves in these mountains that probably no one has ever explored. Perfect places for a fool with gold fever to get lost in. And since we've got the biggest piece of private property around here by far, we get more than our share of treasure hunters, like the two today. The ones *we* catch, they generally get off with just a warning. But according to stories we've heard, a lot worse happens to some."

George laughed. "Sure, Aaron. Or maybe you're just trying to scare us."

Other campers smiled and nodded, but Aaron wasn't smiling.

"I wouldn't joke about it," he said. "Folks really have gotten shot. And others have supposedly headed down into the hollows around here and not come back. There's one old man who lives down the mountain from us—"

"Aaron, stop." Maggie laughed nervously, but he ignored her.

"Let's just say you wouldn't want to be caught treasure hunting on his property. They say he catches copperheads—the poisonous snakes we have around here—and lets them loose on his land. The snakes like to hang out under rocks—same places the treasure hunters like to poke around. Folks in town won't go near his property, and not just because of the snakes either."

"Okay, Aaron, don't make this into a ghost story. Listen, guys," Maggie said to the group, "it's true a few people have vanished around here, but that's got nothing to do with our neighbors. The mountains can just be a little dangerous if you don't know your way around. That's why no one's going off on any crazy treasure hunts." She raised her voice a little. "*Right?*"

"Right," the campers mumbled back.

"Great. Now go pack up and get a good night's sleep. And

make sure you shower before breakfast. It'll be your last one for almost three days. We want to at least *try* to smell better than the bears."

Before Lucas rose from the fire, he noticed that Zack had not returned. Lucas followed Alex and George to their cabin, still wondering what the older boy could be plotting.

CHAPTER 10

When the three boys entered Cabin One, they knew.

A pile of clothes and gear, all of them Lucas's, lay scattered in the middle of the cabin floor. The backpack that had held them—his father's pack—was gone.

"We gotta go tell Maggie," Alex said.

"No," said Lucas sharply. "We find it first. *Then* we'll figure out what to do about Zack."

They headed down the lawn straight for Zack's cabin, but when they peeked in his window, he was nowhere to be found. *Probably watching us from somewhere*, thought Lucas. He thought about yelling out and demanding to know where the pack was but knew that was only what Zack wanted. And there was no way Zack would give up the pack that easily.

They checked the boys' side of the bathhouse next. Lucas half expected to find his pack stuffed in a toilet, but they were all empty, except for one stall occupied by a pair of legs that didn't belong to Zack.

Outside, they checked inside all the canoes and kayaks, but there was still no sign of the pack. Lucas stared out at the water, wondering if Zack had just tossed the pack into the lake, where it might never be found again. Alex and George scanned the water too, obviously thinking the same.

Just then Alex spied something dangling from the zip line, well out over the water.

"Look!" he said in a hushed voice, like he thought Zack might be watching from somewhere close.

Lucas climbed up the zip line platform to get a closer look. Sure enough, a pack was dangling from the harness, which had been pushed a good hundred feet out over the lake.

Lucas immediately started hauling himself out along the cable, hand over hand.

"Whoa, Lucas," said Alex, "what are you doing?"

"What's it look like?" he grunted angrily. "I'm goin' out to get it."

"You'll never make it," said George. "It's way too far out."

Lucas's shoulders tired quickly, so he swung himself a little until he could wrap his legs around the greasy cable and take some of the weight off his arms. He already figured the pack hanging out over the lake was his pa's—what else could it be?—and nothing was going to keep him from getting it back.

By the time he got close enough to recognize the camouflage, his lungs were burning and his shoulders felt like they might pop out of the sockets. He barely had enough energy to hook his legs over the cable for one more rest. When he did, he still couldn't hold on with his aching arms, so he dangled upside down for a while to rest them.

"Jeez," he heard George yell. "Hang on."

"It's just water, George," he yelled back. "And I ain't nearly as high up as you were." He wondered if they'd attracted Zack's attention by now. He imagined the older boy's face pressed up against his cabin window, getting a good laugh at him hanging over the lake in the moonlight.

"Just don't let go, Lucas!" said Alex.

When Lucas finally reached the pack, he realized he'd never make it back using his arms. Instead he pulled the pack from the zip line harness and draped it over the cable long enough to get his legs partly through the harness's leg holes. He reached up and pulled down the pack from the cable just as the harness began moving on its wheels back toward the shore. With the harness only halfway on, he had to hang on to the T-bar to keep from flipping upside down, but he managed to stay upright and hold on to the pack with his free hand as gravity slowly reeled him back to the platform. Twenty feet from the platform, his momentum stopped, and he had to pull himself along the cable with one hand to make it all the way.

When he was over the platform, he tossed the pack down to Alex, untangled himself from the harness, and dropped to the wooden deck. Every muscle in his body felt like rubber as he climbed down the ladder, and he could barely catch his breath.

In the light from the bathhouse windows, the three boys finally examined the pack. What Lucas saw twisted his stomach into a sick knot.

There was a foot-long gash in the bottom, cut cleanly with a knife.

"Jeez, Lucas," said George, "we gotta go get Maggie and Aaron. We can't let him get away with this."

Lucas didn't respond. He just stared at the pack, his jaw clenching with rage.

"Lucas, c'mon," said Alex finally.

"He ain't getting' away with it," Lucas said grimly.

"I know," said Alex. "'Cause we're going to tell Maggie, right?"

Lucas turned to Alex. "No, we ain't."

"What do you mean? Why not?"

Lucas ignored the question. Staring back out at the zip line cable, a plan was already taking shape in his head. "Zack's gonna be up earlier than the rest of us for his breakfast duty, ain't he?"

Alex and George looked at each other, then back to Lucas, nodding.

"I guess," said Alex.

"Then he'll be showerin' in the bathhouse early, by himself, right?"

"Assuming he takes a shower," said Alex.

"*That* pretty boy? He'll definitely take a shower," said George.

"But you heard what Aaron said, Lucas," warned Alex. "You try and fight with him, and you're probably gone."

"And you'd probably get pummeled too," added George.

"Who said anything about fightin'?" Lucas replied. "I got me a better idea."

CHAPTER 11

When the alarm on George's big watch went off, the sky was beginning to brighten, but the sun was still below the crest of the mountains. At the sound of the alarm, Lucas and Alex were on their feet, still dressed from the night before. The high-pitched watch was tucked right next to George's ear, but the younger boy stayed fast asleep until they shook him awake. George fumbled groggily for the right button to silence the alarm. They kept the cabin light off and crept to the front window to begin their stakeout of Zack's cabin. It was the one nearest the bathhouse, the one he now had all to himself thanks to his prank on the zip line.

They didn't have to wait long. Within ten minutes, a light came on in Zack's window.

"Here we go," whispered Lucas. "Y'all remember what you got to do, right?"

"Hey, I'm just back up," whispered Alex. "You guys have

the tough part."

"Just make sure you get to his cabin and lock it up. What about you, George? You ready?"

"I guess," said George nervously.

"You don't sound too sure."

"Jeez, I'll do it, okay?"

"Okay." Lucas was worried about George. He knew the younger kid could handle the talking part of the plan—it was George's idea in the first place—but somehow he doubted George would jump into the middle of a fight with Zack if it came to that.

They watched Zack step out onto his front porch and head for the bathhouse, a white towel slung over his shoulder. Before the door to the bathhouse had even closed, Lucas pushed open their cabin door and jumped silently down onto the dew-covered grass.

The rest of the camp was silent and still, lit only by the light from the bathhouse and a single dim bulb attached to a pole that also held the speaker for camp announcements. Lucas counted on having a good half hour before anyone else, including Maggie and Aaron, woke up.

He sprinted past the fire circle but stopped a few yards short of the bathhouse and crept underneath one of its open windows. Behind him, Alex was already on the porch of Zack's cabin, and he gave Lucas a nervous look before darting inside.

The water in the bathhouse shower was already running, and a moment later, Lucas heard the sound of a shower curtain scraping closed. He waited a few more seconds before opening the door enough to peek in. Just as he'd hoped, Zack's clothes were tossed in a pile on the bench outside the shower. His towel hung on a hook next to the curtain.

Lucas slipped inside the bathhouse. Masked by the sound of the shower, he had Zack's clothes hidden in seconds. But that was the easy part. A few seconds later, he was back outside, waiting for the moment of truth.

Not long after, the water shut off, and the shower curtain scraped again. The next sound was a low growl, like the sound a bear might make before it charges. Zack snarled, "I'm gonna *kill* that dumb hick!"

Lucas eased around the corner and pressed against the wall, peeking just enough to see what happened next. He heard the door on the boys' side open, and Zack appeared, wrapped in his towel and checking for signs of life from the camp. He was about to dash back to his cabin.

Lucas had to muster every ounce of courage to step out behind the bigger kid.

"Dang, Zack," he said, knowing his voice was trembling, "I hope you're plannin' on puttin' on some clothes before you make my breakfast."

Zack turned, fuming at the sight of Lucas. "My clothes.

Now!" he seethed. "Or you're dead."

"I don't know, Zack," Lucas said. "Seems like if we was to start fightin' right here and now, I'd probably be screamin' awful loud. Bound to wake up just about everybody. I'd hate to think what that would look like. You know, me gettin' attacked and all by a naked you."

Lucas grimaced to make sure the ugly image was planted firmly in Zack's head. He was already enjoying Zack's predicament despite the knot in his chest.

"Whatever," Zack sneered. He began walking toward his cabin. "I'll get dressed and *then* kick your butt."

"Oh, see, there's a problem there," Lucas said calmly. "That cabin is all locked up tight by now."

Zack's eyes kept boring into Lucas's, but his shoulders slumped a little. The bigger kid pushed his way past Lucas to search behind the bathhouse. He rummaged for his clothes inside the stacked-up canoes and kayaks, muttering a nonstop stream of curse words and describing in graphic detail the pounding he was about to give Lucas. But the more he looked, the more frantic he became. When he'd searched all of the boats, he moved back toward Lucas.

Lucas stopped him again. "Whoa," he said, putting his hands up in defense. "Look, Zack, I guess maybe I did take this thing a little too far. You can have your clothes back." He motioned over his shoulder toward the lake. "They're right up there."

A towel was tied in a tight bundle and knotted to the zip line, a long way from shore, where his pack had been. Lucas had done it in the middle of the night. He'd hauled himself out in the harness this time and tied the bundle directly to the cable. Of course, they weren't Zack's clothes at all, just a couple more towels bundled inside the first. But by now Zack wasn't exactly thinking straight.

"So go get 'em, redneck," he said.

Lucas pictured his father's pack hanging in the same spot. "Nope," he said, the shakiness finally gone from his voice. "Your turn."

"You're so dead," Zack growled one last time, but he ran toward the lake holding on to the knot of his towel.

In no time, Zack was on top of the platform and stepping into the zip line harness. He didn't bother to tighten the straps, but he had to stop a couple times to keep the towel on. Once he was settled into the harness, Zack's towel was so bunched up around him that Lucas thought it resembled a giant, white diaper.

Zack reached up, grabbed the cable, and began hauling himself hand over hand out to the bundle on the line. When he was halfway there, Lucas heard a faint electric popping as a switch was thrown somewhere in the office.

George's turn, he thought.

Suddenly the sound of the camp bell blasted through the valley.

Zack's blond head twisted around in a sudden panic. He doubled his speed out to the bundle and hoisted himself the last dozen yards. Frantically, he went to work on the knot.

The loudspeakers throughout the camp crackled to life, and the sound of George clearing his throat echoed through the camp.

"GOOOOOOOD MORNING, CAMPERS! WE'VE GOT SOME TOTALLY EXTREME ACTION FOR YOU DOWN BY THE LAKE THIS MORNING!"

Within seconds, the front porches of the cabins were filled with campers, their bleary eyes focused on the half-naked boy suspended from the zip line. Lucas checked the front porch of Zack's cabin and saw Alex leaning out to enjoy the spectacle too.

"IT'S EXTREEEME NAKED ZIP-LINING, STARRING EVERYBODY'S FAVORITE ZIP LINER, ZACK WARREN! C'MON, FOLKS. LET'S SHOW SOME APPRECIATION!"

Over the sudden burst of applause, Lucas heard one girl shriek with laughter while other kids shouted back into their cabins to roust their roommates. One hollered, "Looks like he's wearing a diaper or something!"

While Zack struggled with the knot, Lucas slipped back into the bathhouse and stood on the bench outside the showers. He lifted one of the ceiling tiles and retrieved Zack's clothes from where he'd put them a few minutes before.

Back outside, he laid the clothes out neatly across an up-turned canoe and whistled to get Zack's attention. But when the older boy turned around, the knotted bundle came loose from the cable, throwing him off balance and flipping him upside down. The towels fluttered down to the water. Even worse, the one wrapped around Zack's waist came loose, and he barely snatched it before it dropped from his reach. A roar of laughter rose from the cabins.

"OH NO, CAMPERS!" George gasped dramatically into the microphone. "IT APPEARS ZACK IS IN SOME KIND OF TROUBLE!"

Lucas thought for sure the older boy would tumble into the water, but one leg was still tangled in the harness, so Zack dangled upside down, trying to cover himself with the towel at the same time. Beyond the lake, Lucas spotted Maggie and another counselor heading down the hill toward the cabins. If George saw them too, he didn't let it stop his show. Lucas heard him choke off a laugh before he regained his announcer's voice.

"WHOA!!!" he shouted. "ZACK'S PUTTING ON A GREAT SHOW FOR US TODAY, CAMPERS! IT DOESN'T GET ANY MORE EXTREEEEEME THAN THIS!"

Zack bobbed up and down on the line, frantically claw-ing at the strap tangled around his leg with one hand while covering his privates with the towel. He tried to kick his tangled leg free, but instead began a dizzying spin, bringing more laughter from the cabins.

Finally, still clutching the towel, he slowly descended, upside down, to the platform where he made a clumsy dismount. Free from the harness, he darted behind the lifeguard chair, momentarily trying to hide while he wrapped the towel back around himself before starting down the ladder. Halfway down, the towel slipped off once more, bringing the biggest roar yet from the campers.

"THAT'S ZACK WARREN! BEAST OF THE ZIP LINE! LET'S GIVE HIM A BIG ROUND OF APPLAUSE!"

Zack hopped off the ladder, covered himself again, and stormed toward Lucas, who was pointing at the boy's clothes spread out on the canoe. Zack snatched up his clothes from the canoe and disappeared into the bathhouse. By then, Maggie and the other counselor were coming fast along the lake, but Zack was too enraged to notice them. In ten seconds, he was dressed and charging back out the bathhouse door.

Alex had jumped down from Zack's porch, and he joined Lucas.

"I guess that makes two dead idiots," Zack hissed, taking a step toward them.

Lucas knew it was the moment of truth. "You really gonna fight us both, Zack?"

The question halted the bigger boy's charge, and Lucas kept talking.

"Look, we ain't got no cause to fight no more, Zack, but we will if that's how you want it. The way I see it, we're square for what you done to George. And I might even consider callin' it even on what you done to my pa's pack. You leave us be, and maybe we'll do the same for you."

Zack stood for a few seconds, fists clenched and arms taut, glaring back and forth between the two younger boys. Lucas tried to keep from shaking and braced for the big kid's charge. But suddenly George was at his side too. He was red faced and breathing hard from running down from the office, but he stared Zack in the eye, looking about as mean as a pudgy, freckle-faced twelve-year-old could and letting Zack know he'd have to take on all three of them if he wanted a fight.

Zack stared hard at George, knowing that he was the most vulnerable brick in their shaky wall.

"What are *you* gonna do? Sit on me?"

"Maybe I will," replied George, though it didn't sound too tough.

Suddenly Zack took notice of the two counselors rushing up on them.

"You should get on your knees and thank them," he said, still steaming. "They're the only reason you're all not bleeding right now." He turned toward his cabin.

Lucas grinned at Alex and George and called out to Zack, "Hey, don't forget breakfast." The older boy glared over his shoulder, reversing course toward the path that led up the hill to the dining hall. Lucas watched him go, then turned back to his roommates, laughing out loud, even though the counselors were now within earshot.

"You boys want to tell us what's going on this morning?" Maggie asked sharply. "What was Zack doing up there? And how did you get in the office, George?"

Lucas started to explain, but the goofy grin on his face did little to ease Maggie's anger.

Half an hour later, all three of them were wearing aprons and shoveling out pancakes in the dining room right next to Zack.

CHAPTER 12

By the time they made it back from kitchen duty and packed what they needed for the backpacking trip, the rest of the campers were waiting around the fire ring. In Cabin One, George had made a grunting and groaning spectacle of trying to heft his overloaded pack, so Lucas and Alex sifted through it and tossed everything he didn't need onto his bunk. By the time they left the cabin, the pile included two crushed packages of mini doughnuts, an oversized plastic air mattress, enough bug spray for an army of jungle explorers, and a huge hunting knife. George had whined mightily about leaving behind all of his luxuries, especially the knife, which he claimed he would need for fending off wild animals. But when he shouldered the much lighter pack, he happily forgot his extra gear.

Lucas's own pack was freshly patched with a couple layers of duct tape—something his father had always told him to carry in the field, just like he had in the Marines.

With Aaron and Rooster in the lead, the twelve boys headed up the trail past the dining hall and into the forest. The way out of the valley that morning was not as steep as the trail they'd taken the day before, but it took twice as long to reach the same kind of high, airy views. Around midmorning, Aaron pointed out a worn, wooden Forest Service sign that marked the boundary between camp property and the wilderness area, and soon they were traversing a lofty ridge of lightning-scarred trees and ledges that opened up to vistas across a deep gorge, with another ridge and distant flatlands beyond.

Most of the hikers were carrying big packs for the first time, so the counselors gave them plenty of breaks. Still, the boys made it to the first night's campsite by early evening. The site was a broad, level swath of grass near the top of a rounded knob, and the counselors encouraged the boys to face their tents toward the west in order to see the twinkling lights of the farms and towns down in the valley after dark. With the skies clear, a few campers chose to lay their sleeping bags directly in the meadow and sleep under the stars.

Lucas and Alex finished setting up their tent and helped George with his. Unrolling his sleeping bag, the younger boy complained loudly about the air mattress he'd been forced to leave behind that morning in the cabin.

On the other side of a rock outcrop, well apart from George's tent, Zack unrolled his sleeping bag on the ground. It was a thick bag filled with fluffy goose down, with a luxurious-looking sleeping pad underneath. They had all figured he would keep his distance, and no one was complaining.

"Ah, just like I requested," he said, "a room with a view. He directed his voice toward George's tent. "The air's a lot fresher out here too."

They heard a shuffling from inside George's tent, followed by a tremendous blast of gas. "Smells like a good strategy, Zackster," George yelled. "Besides, you can be my early warning system when a bear comes into camp. When I hear you getting dragged off into the woods, I'll just zip up tight and enjoy the sounds of nature."

"Shoot," said Zack, "any bear that comes up here is going straight for you. To a bear, you're just a big old Twinkie in that sleeping bag—soft on the outside and even softer in the middle."

"Mmm, Twinkies," George replied from his tent.

After dinner, the campers cleared the chunks of charred wood out of an old ring of rocks and built their own fire, sitting on logs rolled into place by campers before them. They talked while the sun dropped below a hazy horizon that seemed a thousand miles away, and the sky fired up into a wash of red and orange that dissolved slowly into the soft blue of twilight. By the time the first faint stars appeared, most of the boys were already in their tents or bundled in their sleeping bags in the grass.

Alex drifted off almost as soon as his bag was zipped, but Lucas lay awake for a long time, listening at first to the rustling sounds of the other boys in their nighttime nests, then to the soft hum of insects in the meadow and the whisper of the night breeze rippling the nylon roof of the tent.

Without the distraction of the other campers, Lucas realized he'd gone the whole day without thinking of his pa. It was the longest he'd done that since the soldiers had come, and it didn't feel right, not thinking about him. A sudden wave of guilt washed over him. *He's the only reason I'm even here, and I forgot him.* He wondered if that was how it would be, his pa slipping further and further away until he'd never remember him again, like he never even had a father. The thought left him lonely and cold. He suddenly longed to touch his pa's backpack, the place where it said *Whitlatch*, but the pack was outside the tent, and he knew the rustling would only wake Alex.

So instead he stared up at the sky through the tent door and listened to a pair of owls calling to each other across the meadow, a cold tear trickling into his ear. Later, when the sky was speckled with a billion stars and the owls had gone silent, Lucas wondered if the owls had found each other or if one had simply vanished into the night.

* * *

They ate breakfast with a bright planet hanging in the hazy pink of the eastern sky and broke camp just as the sun rose.

By midmorning, they were tromping single file across a narrow ridge topped with tilted slabs of rock erupting beside the trail like the petrified fins of some giant, prehistoric dragon. Aaron explained that these were the Preacher Rocks that gave the wilderness area its name.

"Why do they call them the Preacher Rocks?" The question came from somewhere near the front of the line of backpackers.

"Well, if the story is true," answered Aaron, "an old preacher got himself struck by lightning up here. His wife told his congregation that he came up here to get closer to God, but the pick and shovel they found next to his body told a different story. They say he told a friend that he knew for certain that the treasure was up here somewhere in these very rocks. Of course, he never found any treasure. But I suppose he did get closer to God."

George was at the back of the line and spoke quietly, so only Lucas and Alex could hear. "Sounds like a good way to go if you ask me. Nice and quick. I wish my mom had gone like that. Her cancer just shriveled her up like a skeleton. She was pretty much dying for two years."

Neither of the boys said anything at first. These weren't the kind of details Lucas needed to hear, and again he wondered how George could even talk like that about his mother's death.

"My dad says my mom died pretty quick," Alex finally said.

Alex hadn't even wanted to mention his mother just two days ago, so Lucas was surprised that it had come out. Still, he didn't push Alex for details.

Instead, George did it for him. "How'd she die, Alex?"

Alex paused a few seconds before he finally answered. "Car accident. Coming home late from work one night. It was during a big storm. I guess nobody could see too good. They never did figure out if it was my mom or the other guy who crossed the line, but they hit"—Lucas heard Alex's voice catch on the last words—"head-on."

Lucas knew what was coming next.

"What about you, Lucas?" asked George.

"What do you mean?" he replied, knowing exactly what George meant.

"It was your dad, wasn't it?" Alex asked.

"Good guess," Lucas said without offering any details. There were secrets about his family that he wasn't about to let out.

"He was a soldier, wasn't he?" George guessed. "That's where you got the pack, right?"

"Gee, you're a real detective, ain't you, George?"

"Was it in Afghanistan?" Alex asked. "I've got an uncle over there right now."

"Did he get shot?" George asked a little too eagerly.

"Did I even say he died over there?" Lucas responded, an edge to his voice that he hoped would end their questions. He didn't want to invite the images back into his head, but there didn't seem to be any way to keep them out, not with all the talk of dying.

"Sorry, Lucas," said George.

"Look," Lucas replied. "He went quick. A lot quicker'n shrivelin' up with cancer." But then he realized how mean that sounded, so he quickly added. "Sorry, George."

"No. No, you're right," agreed George. "Quicker is better."

George was trying to sound strong—they all were—but Lucas figured George's mind was fixed hard on an image of his mother becoming a skeleton for two long years. And Alex was probably thinking about his mother dying trapped in a twisted car, a rainstorm washing blood out onto the road. But these images were quickly pushed from Lucas's head by an explosion, a smoking wreck, and the screams of soldiers. And his pa running toward the screams down a dusty road. Before he knew it, he was glad Alex and George were behind him, so they couldn't see the tears streaking his face.

CHAPTER 13

A little after noon, the trail entered what seemed like an endless field of boulders. They had to rely on the counselors' memories and occasional cairns, little stacks of stones left by other hikers, to keep them on course. Aaron explained that these would be the last wide-open views of the trip, so they agreed to take a long break and eat lunch. Just after they dropped their packs, Maggie and the first members of the girls' group crested the same knob heading in the opposite direction. They'd already stopped for lunch, so after a few greetings and a quick meeting between the counselors, the girls moved on across the boulder field.

From their lunch spot on top of a truck-sized boulder, Lucas could see across to another ridge paralleling theirs, perhaps a half mile away. The ridge was topped with the same kind of tilted rocks they'd been through that morning. Some of these had broken off from the top of the ridge and tumbled down the cliff face into the trees. Examining these fallen boulders, Lucas spotted a dark depression in the rock face just above the tops of the trees. From where he sat, it looked like it bored straight into the mountainside. Like the mouth of a cave.

He immediately thought of the treasure and how Beale and his men had buried it in their secret mountain vault. Lucas knew it was a stretch, but for all he knew, maybe the preacher had been searching for a cave just like the one he was looking at now.

He elbowed Alex in the arm and whispered, "Check it out. Down at the bottom of those rocks." He didn't point, not wanting the others to see what drew his attention. "What's that look like to you?"

At first Alex didn't see it, but he followed Lucas's eyes to the base of the rocks. "You mean that hole? I thought you saw something good, like a bear or something."

"Shhh. Keep it down." Lucas pointed with his eyes at Aaron and Rooster sitting just a few boulders away. "I don't want them to hear."

"Hear what? About some hole in the rocks?" Suddenly, Alex realized what Lucas was thinking. "You've got to be kidding," he whispered. "There's no treasure in that hole." He looked down into the steep, thickly wooded ravine that separated them from the other ridge. "Even if you wanted to go see it, how would you get over there?"

George looked up from his lunch. "Go see what?" he asked loudly, spitting out crumbs of trail mix.

Lucas rolled his eyes. "Jeez, George, pipe down. There's a cave over in those rocks. Maybe it's what that preacher was looking for."

George peered across the ravine. "Sure, I see it. But if I can see it, so can anyone who ever walked on this trail. It's not exactly a secret, Lucas."

"How do you know?" Lucas asked. "It took us a day and a half to get out this far. And that's only because we came from the camp. Who knows how long it would take from somewhere else. And maybe it's been hidden until one of them fallin' rocks opened it up."

"It'd take like an hour to cross over there and get back," Alex warned. "How are you even gonna get away without Aaron and Rooster knowing?"

Lucas was thinking about it when George spoke up. "Oh, that'd be easy," he whispered. "We could just pretend somebody's gotta go."

"Go where?" asked Alex.

"Not *where*," replied George. "*What*. As in dispose of some hazardous waste. You know, drop the Browns off at the pool?"

Lucas and Alex looked at each other and groaned disgustedly, but George went on. "Like, I could say I gotta go, and you guys are staying behind to make sure I don't get lost. We could even tell them the country boy here is gonna find me the right kind of leaf to use for toilet paper."

"Good one, George," laughed Lucas.

"Whoa, whoa, whoa!" whispered Alex. "Who's 'we'? I'm not leaving the trail. Remember what Aaron said about wandering off?"

"Yeah," Lucas added. "I don't need no help. Y'all would just slow me down anyways."

George shook his head. "But Aaron isn't going to let you stay back on your own. There's no way. And it'd be stupid for us to wait right here when the three of us could all go check out the cave."

"Count me out," said Alex.

"Really, dude?" said George. "Even after Lucas here stood up to Zack for us?"

"For *us!*" whispered Alex. "Don't you mean for *you?*"

"So *I'll* stay back with him. You can cover for us."

"You mean lie."

"Whatever," replied George. He turned to Lucas. "Wanna go for it?"

"Oh, I'm goin', and if y'all want to help, just don't mess it up."

Lucas was feeling the same way he had when he'd decided to get back at Zack—like he didn't care one way or the other if he got in trouble with the counselors. Before his pa died, he'd never been in any real trouble. But now it just didn't seem to matter.

"You know," said Alex, "chasing after that treasure—which isn't even there—isn't exactly the same as sticking up for George. And we'll probably get tossed out of here if they catch us."

Lucas wanted his friends along, but he acted like he didn't even hear Alex. Instead he focused on Aaron and Rooster. They were putting away their water bottles and telling the kids around them to pack up. Soon everyone in the group was rising, stuffing away their trash and shouldering their packs again.

"Whatever," Alex finally said. "What's it matter, anyway?"

Just then Aaron called to them. "Let's go, boys. We've got five more miles ahead of us." A few other boys moaned loudly.

George didn't hesitate. "You mind if I run off to a tree first. I sorta gotta go." Aaron looked skeptical, so George grimaced and did a frantic little dance. "Number two," he added.

Everyone but George, Lucas, and Alex already had their packs on. The other boys groaned at the idea of having to drop theirs again and wait for George.

"Jeez, we've been here like a half hour already," Zack whined, "and you wait till now?"

Before anyone dropped a pack though, George said, "Just

go on. I can catch up. You'll probably want to clear the area first, anyway."

A few of the boys chuckled. "Nasty," added one of them.

Lucas piped up. "Alex and I can stick around with him."

Aaron glanced at Rooster, and Lucas thought for sure he would tell the younger counselor to stay behind with them. But George reached into his pack and pulled out his personal roll of toilet paper. "Boy Scout motto—be prepared," he chirped, turning and winking at Lucas.

The joke seemed to lighten up Aaron.

"Stick together and hurry up. Look for the cairns up ahead. We're not going to slow down for you." He turned back to the front of the line and started walking. "And make sure you bury that stuff," he hollered back over his shoulder.

Alex and Lucas pretended to point out a suitable spot for George to go, but no one was watching. Soon the rest of the boys and Rooster had fallen in line, and the colorful caravan of backpacks began to disappear among the boulders.

Lucas pointed to their own packs lying on the rock next to them. "Leave these right here. That way we'll spot 'em when we come back up and know where to pick up the trail. Y'all ready?"

"I guess we better be, huh?" answered Alex. "Somebody's gotta keep you two from killing yourselves."

CHAPTER 14

The three friends quickly made it down to the base of the cliffs where they'd seen the cave. They scrambled up some fallen boulders until they came to an overhanging slab of rock about a dozen feet from the forest floor. There were plenty of handholds in the little cliff, so they hauled themselves up and over the lip of the ledge until they were facing back into a deep shadow cast by a rock roof. From across the ravine, with the sun in front of them, the overhang's shadow had looked like an endless tunnel, but from here at the opening they could see it wasn't more than twenty feet deep.

Alex took a few steps inside the little cave. "Looks like we aren't even the first here," he called out, pointing to the ground.

A crude fire ring sat far enough under the ledge to be sheltered from the weather. The ceiling above the ring of stones was charred black from smoke, and a few rusted cans were scattered among the ashes. The camp looked like it hadn't been used for a hundred years.

"Could still be where the preacher camped when he was looking for the treasure," offered George.

"I don't know," replied Lucas. "If he'd a had a little shelter like this up here, why would he have been outside gettin' hit by lightnin'?" He moved deeper beneath the rock, until he had to squat to go farther. Suddenly he called out again.

"Dang!" he cried, backing out of the darkness and into Alex.

"What? What is it?" asked George.

Lucas pointed to the back of the cave. "Take a look."

At first they'd looked like only a scattering of bright, white sticks glowing in the gloom. But moving closer, Lucas had recognized them. Bones.

"This is somethin's house," he said. "Whatever it is probably still lives here. Some of these look pretty fresh."

Most of the bones were tiny, while a few others looked like ribs, almost big enough to be human. Whatever used the cave ate everything from mice to deer. A few still had scraps of fur clinging to them, and the dirt around them was stirred up.

"Do you think it's a bear?" George asked.

Lucas squatted next to a long, knobby bone and examined the ground. He whistled under his breath.

"I can't believe it," he said. "Look here."

Alex bent down next to him, but George hung back.

"Four toes and about as big as a baseball," Lucas said, pointing at an arch of round depressions in the dust. "Know what that is?"

"How would we know?" exclaimed George in a hush, like he was afraid someone—or something—might hear. "All I know is it eats meat. And we're meat. *And* we're sitting in its dining room."

Lucas was still mesmerized by the print. "It's a painter track," he said.

"What's a painter?" asked Alex.

"A painter. You know, a big ol' cat 'bout the size of you and me."

"Oh, you mean a panther?"

Lucas laughed. "Painter. Panther. Yeah, same thing. We call 'em painters around home. They's supposed to be long gone from all these mountains. But a lot of folks around my grandpa's say they's still up here. They say they hear 'em some nights. My grandpa even showed me a print once, but even he wasn't too sure. But this here can't be nothin' else. I seen bobcat prints, but this here's way bigger."

"Maybe that print's really old," said George, his voice quaking a little.

"Naw," said Lucas. "The wind would've blowed it away eventually. It can't be older'n a week or two."

"Great," said George. "Can we go now? I'd rather not add my bones to the pile if it's okay with you."

Lucas walked away from the track toward the daylight and began scooting off the ledge to head back. "I don't know, George," he said. "I bet Aaron and them will probably be pretty interested to know they've got a real painter up here."

"Sure," offered Alex, "maybe he'll be so happy he'll go easy with our kitchen duty."

They dropped down the side of the ravine and back into the thick woods, roughly retracing their steps to the other side. Before they were halfway back, Alex spoke up.

"What would you guys do with a treasure like that anyway?"

"That's easy," said George. "I'd open up a whole chain of pizza restaurants all over the country. Each one would have a special table just for me and my friends that no one else could ever sit at. Then I'd buy one of those big luxury campers, the ones that are like the size of a bus, and a driver to take me and my friends to any one of my restaurants, any time we wanted."

"Oh, sure," said Alex, "I'll bet your dad would just let you travel the country with no grown-ups around."

George snorted. "Are you kidding? He'd probably be glad to get me out of his hair. More time for him to spend at work or on the road. Like I said, that's all he does anyway."

"Yeah, but…pizza? That's all you would do with all that money?" asked Lucas.

"Got a better idea?"

Lucas didn't answer at first. He knew exactly what he would do with the treasure, but he wasn't going to let Alex and George in on the sorry state of his life back in Indian Hole.

"I'd think of something," he finally spit out.

"I know what I'd do," said Alex. "I'd buy me a plane. That's what I always wanted to do—fly. Not with someone else doing the flying, but with me at the controls."

"You can't even fly one though," said George.

"Duh. Dude, I'm thirteen," replied Alex. "I can't even drive a car. But with all that money, I could take all the flying lessons I wanted. Heck, I could probably open up my own flight school. In a couple years, I'd be awesome at it."

At the bottom of the ravine, they stepped over a tiny creek not more than two feet wide and climbed up through the trees toward the base of the ledge where they'd started. Alex and George chattered about being rich while Lucas focused on finding the easiest route through the underbrush and back up the rocks to the ledge.

They never saw their three packs—because they were now hidden deep in a dense thicket of laurel on the floor of the forest, far below the rocks.

CHAPTER 15

Half an hour after leaving the panther's cave, the boys pulled themselves up over the last small cliff, expecting at any moment to see the three packs they'd left behind. Instead they saw nothing but rock.

"So where are the packs?" asked Alex.

Lucas looked back at the route they had taken from the cave. He could see the overhang across the ravine. It looked like the same view as when they had first seen it from their lunch spot.

"They's supposed to be right here. I guess we're just off a little."

"But this is where we ate lunch," said George. "This rock. I know it. Our footprints ought to be around here somewhere."

"Ain't no footprints on rocks, George," replied Lucas.

"Then maybe this isn't even where we were! Maybe we're lost!"

"Jeez, George," said Alex. "Give Lucas a chance to think. I mean, we're not lost. Right, Lucas?"

Lucas wasn't too crazy to hear Alex depending on him already, and he was just about sure they were on the exact same ledge where they'd seen the cave, but he put up a good front.

"Yeah, just take it easy, George," he said. "We ain't lost. The packs have gotta be close."

Lucas examined the ground for any sign that they'd been there, but even where the surface wasn't solid rock, it was too gravelly to reveal any prints. In some places, the gravel looked stirred up, but he couldn't be sure. He'd tracked lots of deer back on his mountain, and he knew how to tell plenty of other animals from their prints, but finding a trail across a ridge that was more rock than dirt was a different story.

"Maybe a bear dragged them off," offered Alex. "I mean with all the snacks George was packing in his."

"Sure," said George glumly, "blame the fat kid."

"Naw," said Lucas. "A bear wouldn't have hauled off all three of them. Plus he would've torn 'em up right where they was at. There'd be somethin' left to see. It's all right though. We'll just start looking. They're around here somewhere."

They split up and searched among the boulders for another half hour, always staying within sight, or at least shouting distance, of each other. But there was no sign of the packs. Worse yet, not even Lucas could find anything that looked like a trail across the rocks. Aaron had told them to follow the cairns, but every time Lucas thought he'd found one, it was just a few rocks lumped together, not the neat little stacks they'd seen before.

It was more than an hour since they'd sneaked away, and Lucas couldn't believe that Aaron or Rooster hadn't come back for them. He began to worry that they were so far off the trail they couldn't even hear someone calling. Or maybe one of the counselors had come back when they were still across the ravine and now they were looking somewhere else.

Half an hour later, Lucas gave up looking. He'd even ventured out on his own, far out of earshot, to where the field of rocks ended and the mountaintop turned to forest again. But he returned exhausted and no closer to finding the packs or a trail. It seemed the longer he searched, the more uncertain he was about the way out. If this were his mountain back home, he'd have known exactly where he was and how to get home, but this pile of boulders was nothing like his mountain. He'd relied on someone else to get him out to the middle of nowhere, and now two other kids were relying on him to get them back.

Before long, he saw Alex in the distance, shaking his head and holding up his hands to tell him his luck had been no better. George had stopped looking long before the other two. They found him sitting alone on a rock, wiping tears away with his sleeve. Lucas and Alex sprawled out on the same rock, and for a few minutes, the only sound was George's soft blubbering.

"Sorry, George," Lucas said finally. "Sorry I got you into this. Both of you."

George sniffed and shrugged his shoulders. "It's not like you had to twist our arms. I just can't believe we could get lost so quick."

"What about a person?" asked Alex. "I mean, maybe we're not the only ones up here. Maybe someone's been following us and stole the packs."

Lucas thought about it, but it just didn't make any sense. "What kind of thief is gonna want to carry our packs all the way out of here? Plus, Aaron said we'd probably have the trail to ourselves, and I believe him."

"Maybe not," said George. "Maybe somebody lives close to here. Like that creepy old man Aaron was talking about."

"Aaron said that old man shoots treasure hunters," said Lucas. "He didn't say nothin' about him sneakin' around stealin' backpacks full of kids' dirty clothes and candy bars."

"What about Zack then?" said George. "Maybe he did something with them?"

The thought had already crossed Lucas's mind. "Naw, I definitely saw him up near the front of the line when everyone left. And I watched him the whole way. He never even looked back at us."

"Me too," said Alex. "No way he could have sneaked back here without Aaron or Rooster or somebody seeing him."

"So what are we going to do?" asked George finally. He didn't seem to care that he sounded helpless.

"Anybody got their phone?" asked Alex. "Mine's in my pack."

"Mine too," said George. "It was dragging my pants down when we were walking. What about you, Lucas?"

"Ain't got one." He was looking over Alex's shoulder. "But it looks like the first thing we gotta do is get off these rocks."

"I thought that's what we've been trying to do for the last three hours," whined George in a small voice.

"I ain't talkin' about that. I'm talking about *that*."

Lucas pointed to the west. The sky was a wall of ominous purple, crowned by towering white thunderheads. A breeze that smelled of rain came from the direction of the storm. "That's maybe an hour away," said Lucas. "If we don't wanna end up like that preacher, we're gonna need to be down in the trees somewhere."

"Where are we gonna go?" asked Alex.

"Well, if we can find our way back to it in time, I know one good place to take cover."

"No way, not there," George protested, shaking his head. "There's got to be a better place."

Alex's expression told Lucas that he wasn't exactly thrilled with the idea either.

"Look," said Lucas, trying to calm them down, "that painter's probably miles from here. Even if we don't get hit by lightnin', it's still fixin' to rain buckets. I'd rather be cozy and dry in that hole than mess with a storm up here on top." He pushed himself off the rock and started back to where they would have a view of the other ridge.

Alex followed reluctantly. "*Cozy?*" he said. "You call that cozy?"

George stayed on his rock at first, sniffling and rubbing the last of the tears out of his eyes. "This can't be happening," he muttered. But a low growl of thunder shook the ridge, and a few seconds later, he was following Lucas and Alex back to the ravine.

CHAPTER 16

The storm was on top of the boys much faster than they expected. They had just crossed back over the little creek at the bottom of the ravine when the first big drops began splattering the woods. Halfway up the other side, the trees began to swirl, and the wind roared so loudly they could barely hear each other. Just as hailstones the size of marbles began pelting the rocks, they scurried up to the base of the cliff and dove for the cover of the cave. Within a minute, the hail turned to sheets of blinding rain, and thunder boomed off the ridge so close that Lucas thought it might send a chunk or two of the mountain down on them.

The three boys huddled close to the edge of the cave, just out of the rain. When a bolt of lightning hit so close that the hair on their arms stood up, Lucas and Alex scooted farther beneath the ledge. But George still refused to go back into the darkness where the bones were scattered.

They sat watching the storm for a long time before anyone spoke. "How long do you think this is going to last?" Alex asked Lucas.

"Who knows," answered Lucas. "Maybe a while."

"So what are we going to do?" asked George.

"Only thing we *can* do is stay right here for now. If it lets up quick, we can go back to where we was at, see if anyone's lookin' for us. If it keeps on like this"—Lucas shrugged—"I guess we're here for the night."

"For the night?" asked Alex, laughing nervously. "You're kidding, right? We don't have our sleeping bags or anything."

"Or food," added George

"Well," said Lucas, "I don't think we'll be gettin' too much sleep in here anyhow, so we don't exactly need our sleepin' bags. And water..." He grinned. "We got plenty of that."

He picked up one of the rusty cans left by the fire ring and set it under a steady stream of rainwater pouring off the rock over their heads. Within seconds the can was full, and Lucas rinsed out the rusty mixture and set it back under the stream.

"Wonderful," muttered Alex. "At least *you're* right at home."

The smile dropped from Lucas's face. It was one thing for somebody like Zack to call him a hillbilly, but he didn't expect it out of Alex.

George didn't even notice the sudden change in Lucas.

"Yeah, and what are we gonna eat?" he pleaded. "I'm starving already."

"Dang, George!" replied Lucas angrily. "When *ain't* you hungry!?" He picked up a fist-sized rock and stared at the younger boy. "Besides, the way I see it, if I get to starvin', I got plenty to eat." He looked at Alex. "I mean, me bein' a dirty ol' hillbilly and all, I'm liable to eat just about anything, ain't I?"

"I didn't mean it, Lucas," said Alex. "I guess I'm just pissed at myself for going along with this."

"Yeah, and I'm tryin' to make the best of it," said Lucas. "Look, we ain't gonna die, y'all. We just gotta be smart from here on out."

"But won't Aaron just call for help?" George asked hopefully. "He's got to have a cell phone."

Lucas shook his head. "He probably can't even get a signal in these mountains. And even if he could, there ain't no way somebody's gonna come lookin' for us in this storm. And they ain't gonna be lookin' after dark neither. So we make the best of it and wait for mornin'. Then we—"

"Then we *what*? What if they don't know where to look for us? What if they just find our bones in here a month from now?" George motioned over his shoulder at the back of the cave. "Like those."

"They'll know where to look," said Lucas. "They're gonna

look over where we got lost in the first place. And when they do, we'll be right there waitin' for 'em."

* * *

Three hours later, the wind had eased some, but the rain was still a steady downpour. The storm brought the darkness on quickly, and soon the only light came from the distant flashes of lightning in the east or from George's watch, which blinked on every time he nervously checked the time.

Lucas tried to start a fire by striking the lid from one of the tin cans against a flat rock. Every once in a while he sent a spark or two into the small pile of dry twigs and leaves they'd collected from the back of the cave, but he never got more than a feeble glow.

"Don't matter anyhow," he said, giving up. "Even if I got it goin', there ain't enough dry wood around here to keep a fire all night."

Eventually the boys tried to make themselves as comfortable as possible, lying on the rock slab at the opening of the shelter and staring out into the blowing trees. They were protected from the wind, and the flat rock beneath them still radiated a little warmth from the day's sun. Alex found a long, stout stick and sharpened it by rubbing one end on the rock—in case the panther came around, he said. In the flashes of lightning that lit up their primitive shelter, Lucas told him he looked like a caveman with a spear.

For a good hour, Lucas tried to get comfortable, but between the hard rock, the wind, and worrying about being back on the opposite ridge at first light, he knew he'd never sleep. Eventually Alex fell silent next to him and even George stopped rustling around and moaning about his empty stomach. Just when Lucas assumed both of his roommates had managed to drift off, Alex whispered to him.

"Lucas, you still awake?"

"Yeah." He sat up and looked to where Alex was lying, just a shadowy lump in the dark of the cave. "This rock don't exactly make a great bed."

"I was still wondering about your dad. Like, was he really a soldier?"

Lucas didn't respond at first, afraid of where the talk about his pa might take him. But George shifted in the darkness and prompted him too.

"Yeah, Lucas, did he really fight in Afghanistan?"

Lucas hadn't thought about his father, for the afternoon at least, and now he felt the guilt all over again. He had *wanted* to be distracted at the camp, to have something else to think about besides that terrible moment he'd come out of the woods and seen the soldiers' car—and the days after when he'd learned from his grandparents what had happened to his pa. But it wasn't right, not thinking about him at all. He'd lost his dad's pack, and now he couldn't even keep him in his head. It seemed only right to talk about him now, to say *something* about him, to bring him all the way back to the front of his mind and then some, even if it meant seeing pictures in his head that he wished he'd never see again.

"He wasn't always a soldier," Lucas finally said. "When I was a baby, he was a Scout Sniper in the Marines, but until the mine shut down a couple years back, he was workin' security for the mining company. He always said that protectin' the company's money was a lot safer than diggin' their coal, safer than bein' a soldier even. I guess he seen too many of our kin get killed or hurt bad down there, like my grandpa gettin' his leg crushed. He didn't want me growin' up without no pa."

He picked up one of the sticks he had gathered and tossed it out into the darkness beyond the ledge. "Guess that didn't work out too well."

"So he went back into the Marines?" asked Alex from the darkness behind him.

"Not at first," replied Lucas. "When the mine closed, it pretty much killed the town near us, so there weren't any real jobs around Indian Hole. So my pa started leaving me with my grandpa and grandma a lot. He'd work all week in Charleston or Bluefield—those are the bigger towns a few hours from Indian Hole—and then come home on the weekend to see us. But then the Marines started offerin' good money for people like him, people with his kind of experience. He figured

114

if he was gonna be away from home anyway, it might as well be for better money." Lucas stopped for a second and rubbed at his eyes. "Left the day after Christmas."

"I bet your mom hated him being gone so long," said George. "My mom always hated it when my dad was working on the road, and he wasn't ever gone more than a week."

Lucas snorted out half a laugh. "I ain't got a ma. Never had one, really. Supposedly she ran off when I was about a year old, the first time my pa was in the Marines."

"Jeez, that's terrible, Lucas," said George softly.

"It's all right. Heck, it's probably why me and my pa got along so good. Maybe 'cause we kinda needed each other." Saying it made Lucas's eyes well up again, and suddenly he had to swallow hard to keep his voice steady.

"He had me when he was pretty young, so sometimes it was almost like havin' a big brother instead of a pa. And I ain't got no brothers or sisters, so we did a lot together, just me and him. He taught me how to shoot when I was little, so we hunted together since I was maybe eight or so. And we got us a good-sized creek down at the bottom of our mountain, so we used to fish a lot too."

The tears were running down his cheeks now, so he was glad when George spoke up again. In the darkness, his voice sounded lonely and far-off, like he was lost in memories of his own. "Sounds like you had a way better dad than me, Lucas."

Lucas listened as a gust left over from the storm shook the rain from the trees outside the cave. "Maybe," he said.

The younger boy laughed, but there was no smile in his voice. "Seriously. All that stuff you did together? My dad never does that stuff with me. Never has, never will. He's all about work. Twenty-four seven. Most of the time he's on the road too. I guess it just didn't matter so much to me when my mom was alive, but I was stupid enough to think he'd change. Like maybe somehow he'd need *me* more or something."

His voice cracked when he said the last part, and it was a few seconds before he started up again. "Now he says he's got to work even more because we don't have her to help with the money. But that's bull. I think he just wants to avoid me or something. I know it's not the same as you, Lucas, but sometimes I feel like both of *my* parents are gone too." He sniffed back his tears and added, "At least when your dad went away, it was to take care of you."

Alex had been listening quietly. "So he never came back, did he, Lucas?" he said.

Lucas didn't respond at first—not just because the answer was obvious, but because the words cut him even deeper somehow, lost like he was in the dark and lonely mountains.

"Well," said Alex, "I bet he at least died like a hero, Lucas. Beats getting killed in some stupid car wreck like my mom."

He knew exactly how his pa had died, but he'd never told

it to anyone. But now, it was as if the dark loneliness of this one night was focusing the terrible pictures in his mind so starkly that he had to tell someone just to rid his head of them. Way in the east, lightning flashed, too far now to hear the thunder.

"Yeah, he *was* a hero," he began, knowing he'd never get it all out without bawling but not caring any more. "That's what them two soldiers even told my grandma the day they come up our road to tell us. That's all they could say, but we learned the rest later. That he was in a convoy, and I guess he rolled right past a bomb set up in a junked car next to the road." He paused to wipe his eyes with his T-shirt.

"Funny thing is, that one didn't get him. But it got the truck behind him." His voice was already breaking and he was having trouble getting a full breath of air, but he forced the words out. "He was...supposed to wait for the bomb guys to come...and check for more bombs in the road, but... but they said he couldn't stand to hear the screamin' from the guys in the truck...Those were his friends back there. So my pa...he just ran." As Lucas said it, he saw his father's face more clearly than he had since the day of the soldiers.

"He ran to help his friends!" The last part of it came choking out of him, and he put his face in both hands and sobbed.

George and Alex didn't say anything, and it was a full

minute before Lucas could speak again. When he did, he was still crying some, still choking on his breath.

"He got killed…by a bomb right there in the road…All we got to see of him…was a coffin with a flag on top of it…" It was a picture he'd never shake, that and the little movie in his head, the one of his pa running down a sandy road toward a burning truck.

"So he *was* a hero, Lucas," said George quietly. "A real hero."

Lucas sniffed and sucked in a shallow breath. "Yeah, he was," he said, "and I wish he'd been a coward."

He stood up, wiping his nose with his arm, and paced to the other side of the ledge. He wasn't talking so much to Alex and George now as he was to the black wilderness itself.

"I mean, why'd he always have to worry about someone else? Like goin' off to fight. That wasn't for him. He said that was so I'd have choices. Well, you know what choice I woulda made? I woulda chose a pa who ain't dead!" He yelled it out at the forest, but it was his pa he was screaming at now, and he knew it. "Just…one…stupid…time! Why'd you have to worry about somebody else!? You shoulda been worryin'… about *me*!"

His last words echoed out of the mouth of the cave and died out in the blowing trees. Lucas sat down hard on the rocks and drew his knees up close to his face. After that, there was only the sound of the wind and his tears.

CHAPTER 17

When he finally stopped crying, Lucas lay back on the rock, his arms folded over his eyes. He knew he'd embarrassed himself in front of George and Alex, but somehow he felt better for it, like something that had been trying to bust out of his skull for months was finally gone. It suddenly came to him that he'd never felt so tired in his life. It was late now, probably after midnight, and the hiking had tired him out good. But it was spilling his guts about his father that had drained the last drop of energy from him.

Alex sensed that it was okay to speak again. "I'm sorry I asked, Lucas," he whispered.

"Yeah, we won't talk about it anymore," George added.

"Nobody made me tell it," said Lucas, his voice steadier now. "And maybe I'm glad I did anyway."

"So I guess you'll be living with your grandparents for a while, huh?" asked Alex, eager to change to subject.

Lucas laughed. Who else was he going to live with? The only question now was *where*.

"What's so funny?" asked George.

"Yeah, I'll be living with them. Fact, we're gonna have a lot of money too. Not as much as our ol' buddy Zack I bet, but enough that I'll be livin' in a real house somewhere."

"Why's that?" Alex asked.

"'Cause my grandparents are sellin' our mountain to the minin' company. And then it's gonna get torn up so bad my pa probably won't even recognize it when he looks down from Heaven.

"Shoot," he went on, "I guess now you know why I didn't feel like talkin' about no buried treasure yesterday. Y'all want pizza and airplanes. Heck, I'd take that money and get us that real house too. Maybe one with a room just for me, with a real bed like I used to have. And I'd get us a truck that ain't rusted full a' holes too. And some real doctorin' for my grandpa's leg. But most of all, I'd save our mountain from bein' torn to hell. That's what my pa wanted, and it's the only thing I know I want for sure. Ain't exactly some rich kid's dream, is it?"

It wasn't the only reason he'd refused to talk about the treasure. He knew that hatching some fantasy about the rest of his life would only force him to wonder about his *real* future—a hole that right now was only getting deeper and darker, threatening to swallow him up forever.

Just then, a long scream split the darkness.

It was distant but clear, rising over the wind. It sounded like a woman in terrible pain, crying out for help.

Lucas knew immediately what it was, but from the cave in the mountains in the middle of the night, it was the scariest sound he'd ever heard.

Alex jumped to his feet and scrambled for his stick, and George whispered, "Holy crap!"

Lucas didn't even sit up. "Y'all hear that?" he asked, trying to sound calm.

"Of course we did!" replied Alex. "What was it!?" Like George, he was whispering, as if whatever made the noise would somehow hear him, even from far away.

Lucas sniffed the last of his tears away. "The painter, I guess." He was thankful the big cat had screamed when it did. No more talk about parents, at least not tonight.

"You mean the same thing that left those tracks?" Alex said in a panicky voice. "In here?"

"My grandpa told me they sound just like a woman screamin'. That's about the only thing it could be."

"Guys," whispered George, "I think I peed in my pants. Seriously."

Alex ignored him. "Maybe it's somebody yelling for us, back on the other ridge."

"Nope," said Lucas, "ain't nobody up here in the dark. If

they was, we'd have seen their lights over there. Besides, that didn't come from over where we was at. More like from up behind us somewhere." He got up and stood at the opening of the cave, listening for another scream.

"Great!" said George, the panic rising in his hushed voice, "It's probably coming back home from a night of hunting. And we're sleeping in its bedroom!"

"Naw, even if it is comin' this way, it'll smell us in here way before it gets too close. That'll be enough to keep it away."

"And what if it doesn't?" asked Alex.

Lucas sat down next to him, still facing the dark forest in front of the cave. "Then I guess we got one more reason to stay awake."

The panther screamed again, clearer this time. Lucas felt the hairs stand up on the back of his neck, but this time it was more from the thrill of hearing it than any fear.

"That was closer, wasn't it?" George asked.

Lucas didn't respond. Instead he stepped over to the fire ring and started collecting some of the smaller stones. He placed them in a small pile where the others were sitting, and he sat again.

"What are those for?" asked George.

"Look, y'all," Lucas said calmly, "that painter ain't comin' around here tonight. But just in case he does, all we got to do is make a lot of noise and throw a few rocks at him. My grandpa's always said they's pretty much scaredy-cats, especially if more'n one person's around."

Alex grabbed a fist-sized rock in his throwing hand and held his makeshift spear tight in the other. He sat down next to Lucas, the three of them waiting to hear the scream again.

When they finally did, it was even closer. In fact it seemed to come from the ridge just above them.

"I thought you said it wasn't coming around here tonight," George whispered frantically.

"It just ain't smelled us yet, that's all," said Lucas. "It don't know we're down here. The wind's blowin' from behind him, right over the ridge and out into these woods." He picked up a couple more rocks from the fire ring. "But I guess it'd be smart to keep at least one pair of eyes peeled all night. I can take first watch."

He tried to sound brave, but as much as he wanted to see a real live painter up close, seeing one from a pitch-black cave in the middle of nowhere wasn't his first choice. He knew he wouldn't sleep much anyway, if at all.

"I'll stay up with you, Lucas," said Alex, moving closer to his friend.

"Me too," said George. "I'm too hungry to sleep anyway."

"Sure," said Alex, "too hungry. That's it."

"Shut up," replied George. "I'm serious."

For the next half hour they sat quietly, listening for the

panther. It screamed only once more, above them again but more distant. Not long after, Lucas heard George's breathing change, and he knew the younger boy had drifted off. Minutes later, Alex lay his stick down and fell asleep too.

For another half hour, Lucas stared into the shadows at the edge of the cave. Far on the horizon, out over the tidewater or maybe even the ocean, the lightning from the storm still flashed dimly. Finally, he lay back on the rock and watched the clouds above him drift apart to reveal a dense blanket of stars. The forest became still enough to hear the soft buzzing of the insects, and long before the sky began to brighten in the east, he fell asleep and dreamed, for the first time in months, of him and his father, together, down by the little creek below the trailer.

CHAPTER 18

In the morning, the three boys climbed up to the ridge above the cave. A pocket of mud between the rocks held a single panther track, confirming that the big cat had been just above them for at least part of the night. There was no sign of it now, but with evidence so fresh, even Lucas couldn't shake the feeling that the panther was close, eager to reclaim its den from the three intruders.

They agreed it made no sense to stay in the cave, and with the fresh track right where they stood, Alex and George were anxious to move on.

"We could go back over and try to find the trail again," Alex suggested. "If they're looking for us, that's where they'll end up."

"So where are they then?" countered George. "And we looked for the trail for hours over there yesterday. We keep looking, and we could end up even more lost on that side."

Even from this distant vantage point, it was impossible to tell where the trail crossed the boulders.

"What do you think, Lucas?" asked Alex.

"I'm for gettin' out of here, one way or another," Lucas said. "I ain't scared of no painter, but it could be a while before anybody comes lookin'."

"What do you mean?" asked George.

"Well, Aaron and Rooster weren't supposed to get back to the camp until today some time. Even if one of 'em started hurryin' back, it could be pretty late before word gets out. If there ain't enough day left, they might not start lookin' for us till tomorrow morning."

"Great," said George, sounding like he might start crying all over again.

Lucas scanned the other nearby ridges, but there wasn't a single sign of civilization. The valleys to either side of their ridge were blanketed in thick folds of forest for nearly as far as he could see. But far below in the morning haze, he spied a few openings of pasture and a handful of buildings.

He turned back to the others. "There's that little stream we crossed in the bottom of the ravine. It's got to flow into something bigger. If we just keep followin' water, we're bound to end up on *someone's* farm. Can't be more'n five or six miles out of these mountains. We'd probably be at a house with a phone by the time Aaron and them even got back to camp."

"Five or six miles," groaned George. "Are you kidding me?"

"It's all downhill, George," Alex said. "I say let's get moving. Besides, we're never going to find a real meal standing around up here."

George shot him a look. "Really? Food? You really think that's all I think about?"

Lucas and Alex looked at each other, smiling for the first time in a day.

"Whatever," George conceded, "let's just go." He began walking back toward the ravine.

"Don't worry, George," said Alex. "I bet Lucas here can rustle you up some roots and berries along the way. Maybe even a tasty bug or two."

"Fantastic," muttered George.

They clambered back down the rocks and into the damp forest. In a few minutes, they'd found the stream, but before they started to follow it, Lucas stopped them.

"Wait a second," he said. "I think we ought to go back up to where we thought the trail was and leave some kind of message. You know, if they come lookin' up there."

The others agreed, so they climbed the opposite side of the ravine once more. Up among the boulders again, Lucas picked up a sharp stone and handed it to Alex.

"Here," he said. "My writin' probably ain't as good as yours. Especially with a rock."

"What should I write?" Alex asked.

Lucas thought for a second. "How 'bout 'downstream' and then scratch an arrow pointin' that way." He pointed down the valley where the little creek flowed.

Alex scrawled the word into the flat side of a big boulder in foot-high letters. Under it, he scratched a long arrow. He had to go over the whole thing three times to make it stand out enough that a searcher might see it. Still, it was hardly visible from more than a few yards away. So they gathered several large stones and piled them into a crude pyramid on top of the message rock.

"Maybe that will get their attention too," said Lucas.

The three boys stood up and looked at their handiwork. To Lucas, the signal still looked lost in the wide boulder field. Alex must have been thinking the same thing. "Well, I guess it's something," he said.

They worked back to the creek and began picking their way downstream. At first, the walking was easy. The little creek had only cut a small rut through the woods, and the forest floor along its side was level and clear. But when the mountainside steepened, the tumbling watercourse exposed boulders, and the boys had to probe their way more slowly.

In less than a mile, the creek joined a slightly larger stream, and the forest around it grew thicker with tangles of dark evergreens. Soon they were alternating between both sides of the stream and the water itself, whichever offered the easiest path.

Lucas's boots were quickly waterlogged, but he didn't care. He just wanted off the mountain.

After a couple miles, the stream became deep enough that they began to spot small trout in some of the little pools. They stopped at one pool long enough to watch the fish. They were only five or six inches long but colorful, their moss-colored sides shimmering with golden spots.

"At least if we really got stuck here, we'd have somethin' to eat," observed Lucas.

"Yummy," grumbled George, "raw fish."

Even though Lucas hadn't eaten in nearly a day, he had to agree with George. But watching the trout hover in their crystal pool sparked the thirst in his throat. Alex must have been feeling the same way because he started to scoop some of the creek water to his lips. Lucas stopped him.

"I wouldn't do that if I was you."

"Why? It's springwater, isn't it?" Alex protested. "People pay three bucks a bottle for this stuff at home."

"It might be safe, but even mountain water's got some bugs that'll get in your gut and make you wish you was never born. You'd make it out of here, but you'd probably spend the next week on the toilet. I wouldn't chance it. Least not yet."

"How do you know all this stuff?" George asked.

Lucas shrugged. "Heck, what else am I supposed to know about?" He spread his arms out wide. "I mean, I got a mountain just like this here in my backyard."

Just saying it reminded him of what he stood to lose. Losing the mountain, like losing his pa, was like losing a part of him. He knew every game trail and every spring. Knew where the old stone foundations of his ancestors' cabins sat with hundred-year-old trees growing smack in the middle of them. He knew the darkest parts of the forest, where the best mushrooms sprouted and where the thickest patches of huckleberries grew at the edges of meadows near the top. He knew the best climbing trees and the outcrops of ancient granite where a boy could lie for hours on the warm rock and watch hawks drifting overhead or listen to the chatter of ravens. Now there'd be no use for knowing any of it.

"Yeah, but there's kids in my school from the country," said George. "They're not all that smart about the woods and stuff. Not like you are."

Lucas gazed around at the forest. "I don't know. I guess my pa taught most of it to me. They said nobody knew them mountains like him. And he was a scout in the Marines, so he was used to bein' out on his own, findin' his way around. That was how he said he liked it. But he said a lot of it was stuff my grandpa taught him, and *his* pa taught him. And a lot of it, well, he said it was in our blood, knowin' our way around the wilderness. My grandpa says it's the Indian blood in us, from way back when one of my kin married one of the last Indians livin' in our mountains." He looked around at the deep hollow they were in. "'Course, right now, I ain't so sure it's doin' us much good."

They left the pool and dropped deeper into the hollow. Even though the sun was now high in the sky, their surroundings seemed to get gloomier with every step. The farther down the mountain they went, the higher and thicker the trees grew, darkening the forest floor. Once, when a branch snapped nearby and something large crashed through the brush, even Lucas nearly jumped out of his skin. But it was only a whitetail buck, scared up out of the stream by the boys' noisy progress. The deer bounded off, and in seconds, only his snowy tail was visible, dancing away in the dim forest like a tiny ghost.

Half an hour from the trout pool, they heard falling water below them, and soon they were standing at the top of a noisy waterfall that dropped twenty feet into a jumble of moss-covered boulders. Lucas suggested they skirt the drop by using a sloping ledge along one side of the ravine. Alex and George agreed. It was the only way down without heading back uphill to find another route past the fall.

Inching their way sideways along the ledge, they used their fingers to feel for holds in the rock. Lucas led the way, concentrating on where to put his hands and feet but mostly just hoping the steep ravine would let up soon so they could make quicker progress. He reached up to grab the lip of a small ledge, testing it for a handhold, and checked behind him to see if Alex and George were making the same downward progress.

Just then, Alex yelled, "Lucas! Stop!" His eyes were wide and fixed on the ledge Lucas was gripping.

Lucas followed his friend's terrified gaze and slowly leaned back enough to see the top of the ledge. An inch from his own shifting hand, camouflaged perfectly against the wet leaves and rusty pine needles, a copperhead was coiled on the rock.

CHAPTER 19

Lucas started to withdraw his hand, as slow as possible, but the snake was already poised to strike. It tried to slither backward but had no room to escape. It kept its head pointed straight at the fingers that had invaded its mossy bed.

Lucas gasped. He pressed his face against the rock, thinking that hiding part of himself from the snake would calm it down. With his head turned downstream, he began to slowly ease his hand of the ledge, imaging the snake's fangs sinking into his fingers at any moment. From behind him, Lucas heard George whisper frantically, "Alex! No!"

Lucas turned just in time to see Alex swinging a flat rock down on the snake.

Alex aimed for the snake's wide head, but his blow hit mostly rock and sent a tiny splinter of stone bouncing off Lucas's forehead.

The stunned snake flattened itself against the ledge, a drop of blood on its neck. It pulsed with anger and frantically wriggled the tip of its tail like a rattler, a sure sign it would strike. But Alex was already raising the rock for another blow.

"No! Leave it!" Lucas yelled, but it was too late.

Alex brought the rock down again, and the snake struck his hand.

Jerking away, Alex lost his balance. He tilted back from the boulder, grabbing for it, but kept falling. With one foot, he pushed away from the rock, trying to make a clean jump, but there was no safe place to land in the jumble of jagged boulders and shallow water below. Lucas heard a sickening snap when Alex landed.

"*Aaaagh!*" Alex toppled over onto a rock and grabbed at his ankle. He looked frantically up at the others on the ledge. "Where'd the snake go?" he yelled, his face twisted into a mask of pain.

"It's up here still, right next to my foot!" hissed George. Lucas looked down. The snake had dropped to the ledge between them and coiled up again. Its eyes were angry yellow slits, and its black tongue flicked in and out rapidly, probing the air for the predator it had just bitten. Its head was bloodied.

George started to scurry backward, muttering a string of curse words.

"Just freeze!" hollered Lucas. "Don't move! It's a copperhead. Let it calm down and it'll leave."

George stopped moving, but Lucas could hear his breath coming in gasps.

Finally, after what seemed like forever, the snake slowly uncoiled. It wriggled off the ledge and disappeared beneath the boulders, leaving spots of blood on the rock. Lucas figured it would be dead before long.

He started working his way down the rock to his injured friend. "It's gone," he told Alex. "How bad are you hurt?"

Alex was sitting on a rock, sucking hard on the side of his hand and spitting. He stopped and used his good hand to cradle the one with the bite. When he looked up at the other boys, his face had gone pale, and his eyes had a lost look that made him seem very small.

"I think it got me," he said. "My thumb is burning!" He started to get up but screamed again and collapsed on the rock. "And my ankle is messed up."

Lucas crouched down and examined Alex's hand. The thumb was red and swelling a little, but Lucas could see only one puncture mark. "I think it only got you with one fang. That's good."

"Maybe, but it hurts like you know what." Alex tried to croak out a laugh. "But at least it'll keep my mind off my ankle." He moved the foot a little and grimaced again. Then he folded his arms across his knee and buried his face.

George was still frozen up on the ledge. "What are we going to do?"

Lucas knew it was all his fault they were stuck in the middle of nowhere, and now Alex was hurt, but he was still getting sick of the younger boy's whining.

"I guess *I* gotta go for help," he snapped at George. But he changed his tone for Alex, trying to sound optimistic. "Look, I'll get down the creek as fast as I can and find a house." He tried to sound confident, but he sure didn't like the idea of continuing down the mountain alone, not with the luck they were having. "George can stay here with you."

"What!?" exclaimed George.

"George, listen!" snapped Lucas again. "He's hurt. Someone's got to stay with him, and someone's got to go get help. Alone."

Lucas hated the sound of the word, but it got the message across to George.

"No problem. You go. I'll stay with Alex."

"You can't go fast," said Alex through his tears. "It won't do anybody any good if you get hurt too."

"But what about the snakebite?" asked George. He wasn't going to say it, but they knew what he was asking. *Would the bite kill Alex?*

Lucas saw that more of Alex's hand already looked a little puffier. "It ain't gonna kill him, but his hand's gonna hurt bad."

"Already does," said Alex, closing his eyes tight.

"I know. I'll go fast. I promise."

Alex struggled to smile. "Watch for snakes."

Not funny, thought Lucas, a sharp panic already setting in. He turned to scramble down the mountain on his own.

* * *

Below the falls, Lucas made better progress. The image of his friend lying in pain upstream pushed him faster than he knew he should go. *Follow the stream and find a house*, he told himself. *Don't think of nothin' else.* Negotiating the tangle of shrubs and slick boulders demanded enough concentration that he was almost able to keep his mind off still being lost, but now alone.

For nearly an hour, the going was slow. But then the hollow that carried the stream began to flatten a bit, and every once in a while, he even caught a glimpse of green farmland down through the trees. For the first time since they'd left the mountaintop, Lucas began to think he was leaving the worst of it and getting closer to civilization.

As he picked his way along the bank of the small stream, Lucas remembered something his father had told him that last day before he went away. About how a man's life was like their little creek back home—not much more than a trickle at first, but fresh and full of energy. And that the rough spots, like him having to go off and fight, were like the dangerous rapids and waterfalls downstream when the creek turned into a real river. But the rapids go by quick, he'd said, and after a while, everything smooths out like the way it's meant to be, like a river's long and quiet run across the flatlands to the ocean.

Five minutes later though, the growing roar of more falling water ahead reminded Lucas he was still smack in the middle of a rough spot.

Soon he was standing at the top of a rock wall nearly three stories high. The stream spread out in a watery sheet that draped down the nearly vertical face, covering it in a treacherous layer of slippery green algae. Below the waterfall lay a dark pool, too deep to see the bottom.

Lucas looked along the edges of the fall for a safe way down, but the dank shade of the hollow and the constant mist from the falling water had created a snarl of brush-covered boulders that looked impossible to navigate.

There was no time to find a way around. Somehow he had to descend the falls.

Easing himself backward over the edge, he found a dry foothold and wedged his hand into a crack. The crack continued a good ten feet down, clear of the water. He made use of it to get nearly halfway down the face of rock. There, he was able to get both feet onto a tiny ledge and rest. He hugged the rock and peeked down over his shoulder. The rest of the descent wouldn't be so easy.

Lucas inched his way sideways along the ledge, searching by feel for a new handhold. He blindly explored a new crack with his hand, trying to convince himself that no snake would make a home in such a steep and waterlogged cliff, but his trembling legs weren't so convinced. Only the need to help Alex kept him moving.

With his face pressed against the cold, moss-covered rock, he got his fingers into the crack and then found a place for his right foot farther down. He took one hand out of the crack to shake some feeling back into it. When he did, a few more pounds of his weight shifted to the new foothold.

The rock collapsed beneath his foot.

Lucas yelled and clawed at the cliff with his free hand, but the lunge only dislodged his other foot. He swung out over the pool, momentarily suspended by one hand. In the half second it took to realize he was going to fall, he pushed away from the rock with his leg, aiming for the deepest part of the pool below. He screamed as he fell, pitching over sideways. He smacked the pool with the side of his face, and all the sounds of the world disappeared from his ears.

For an instant, everything was black, and Lucas was certain he was dead. Then he felt the freezing shock of the water.

Disoriented, he probed for the bottom of the pool with his legs but found no resistance. He reached out blindly and his hand met a thick branch covered in slime. Not knowing which way was up, he hoisted himself away from the branch, and his head broke the surface of the pool.

He pulled himself half out of the water and flopped over onto his back. He examined the side of his face for blood or a lump but found neither. Still, the roar of rushing water in his ears sent an electric jolt of pain through his jaw and forehead, and for a moment, he thought the fall had deafened him.

Lying next to the pool, the blurry wash of green above him slowly became a canopy of trees. He felt the wet, rounded rocks beneath him and the cold water seeping through his boots. He was just about to sit up when something pointy and hard prodded his shoulder. When he reached up to brush it away, he heard a gravelly voice, one that he remembered instantly.

"This ain't no public swimmin' hole, boy."

Lucas turned and squinted through the pain behind his eyes.

It was the old man. The one from the store. The one from Aaron's story who planted copperheads in his hollow.

The snake man.

He was poking Lucas with the barrel of a shotgun.

CHAPTER 20

"I fell," Lucas said groggily. He pulled himself up onto his elbows, keeping one eye on the gun and the other on the old man behind it.

"Fell? From up there?" The man waved the shotgun at the top of the falls. A small, brown spider crawled across his matted, white beard, but the old man didn't seem to notice. "You oughta be dead."

"Not from the top. I was climbin' down and I slipped. I hit the water. Hard." He fingered the side of his face again and wiggled his jaw, wincing.

If the old man felt any sympathy for him, he didn't show it. He kept the shotgun pointed at Lucas while he talked. "Who you with, boy? Better yet, why you trespassin' on my property?"

Trespassing. Lucas recalled what the clerk in the store and Aaron had told them about what the snake man did to trespassers. How some people had wandered into these woods and disappeared.

"My friends and I got lost. We were at the camp. Camp Kawani. We got lost on a hikin' trip." He wasn't going to say anything about looking for treasure. But the old man didn't buy his story anyway.

"Kids from that camp don't just get lost. You a runaway?"

"No. We just…took a little side trip. We lost the trail. We were stupid. We shoulda stayed with the group."

The old man finally pointed the shotgun away from Lucas, cradling it in his other arm. It was big, an old twelve-gauge pump, but it seemed weightless the way he handled it. Even with the barrel pointing the other way, Lucas didn't feel any safer.

"Stupid sounds about right. That camp's been over there near twenty years, and they ain't lost a kid yet. Not till now at least. So where're these friends of yours?"

"They're upstream. Maybe a mile. No more'n two. One of 'em can't walk. He broke his ankle or something. And a snake bit him. A copperhead."

Lucas watched the old man's eyes when he said the last part. He wondered if the lunatic holding a gun on him had put Alex's snake in the hollow too.

The old man's expression didn't change. "I guess you and your friends managed to get yourselves in a heap of trouble."

The way he said it made Lucas shiver, not knowing if the old man meant the trouble they'd already had or what they had coming. Still, the old man was his only chance of getting help for Alex and George.

"We have to go back up there and get them."

The man laughed. "*We*? What do you think, boy, I'm gonna *carry* your busted-up friend out of here? It's already a hard couple miles back down to my place, and that's just from *here*. Best just to get you out of here while we got some daylight. Then maybe we'll worry about your friends."

Lucas's anger started to grow. Was this old man really planning to leave Alex injured and stranded for the night?

"What do you mean, *maybe*? They can't spend the night up there. If you can't do it, then I'll get them down as far as this waterfall. They're not too far. You could go back and get someone to meet us here."

Lucas knew he could never get Alex down to the waterfall by himself, even with George's help. He wasn't even sure he could climb back up the creek, as hungry and exhausted as he was. He hoped the old man would take it as a challenge, like Lucas was telling him again that he was feeble, that he needed a kid to help him out. He remembered the angry reaction he'd gotten in the store.

The man stared back upstream, perhaps weighing whether or not to leave the other boys. Lucas had to stand his ground.

His friends were counting on him to bring help. He couldn't leave them alone at night in the wilderness, wondering if he had abandoned them.

"Look," he said defiantly, "I'm not going anywhere unless I get my friends out of here. *Today.*"

The old man turned slowly and stared at him. He threw the shotgun back over one shoulder and twisted a tuft of white beard between his fingers, his cold eyes locked on Lucas's. Finally, he spoke.

"Sassed me just like that in Herschel's store not four days ago, didn't you."

Lucas wasn't going to back down now. "Yes, sir. You were rude to my grandma."

The old man smiled wryly. He took the shotgun off his shoulder, cradling it, and Lucas thought he'd crossed a line. *I'm dead,* he thought, *just like the missing treasure hunters.*

Instead the old man racked the shotgun until all the shells were on the ground. He pocketed them and leaned the gun against a fallen tree.

"Stay here and keep your hands off my gun."

Then the old man climbed up the rocks of the waterfall like he'd done it a hundred times, cursing under his breath the whole way up.

* * *

The woods were darkening with long shadows when Lucas

heard the old man returning with Alex and George. He couldn't see them coming from the foot of the steep waterfall, but there was no mistaking Alex's arrival. His painful moans grew loud enough to hear over the falls, and Lucas was suddenly fearful of seeing what terrible shape Alex might already be in.

Lucas heard the old man grumble something at his two friends before he peered over the top of the falls.

"Best climb up here, boy," he yelled over the splashing water. "We ain't goin' back to my place that way. Not with this one at least."

Lucas pointed at the shotgun leaning next to him. "What about your gun?" he called back.

"Leave it. I saw what you done to yourself tryin' to climb this rock. I'd surely hate to see the same happen to my gun."

Lucas quickly started climbing back up the waterfall, taking the route the old man had followed. Going up wasn't nearly as tricky, and he made steady progress, but not without catching grief for moving too slow.

"Let's go, boy," the hermit hollered at him from above. "I already hauled your friend halfway down this mountain! I ain't haulin' you up that rock!"

When Lucas finally made it up the falls, the sight of Alex made him wince. His friend's hand was swollen past the wrist, and his thumb had turned almost purple. The old man had used a pair of stout sticks and some kind of vine to splint Alex's foot, but now that his boot was off, Lucas could see that the foot was badly swollen too. Streaks of dried tears marked Alex's dirty face. Still, he managed a weak smile when he saw Lucas.

"Thanks for finding...help, Lucas," he said.

George was still picking his way down the rocks along the stream, making much slower progress than even the old man with a boy on his back. He was carrying Alex's boot in one hand. When he spotted Lucas, his wide-eyed glance toward the old man revealed his fear.

"I didn't find him. He found me." Lucas kept his voice low, watching the old man resting against the trunk of a tree. "All I managed to do was fall off this waterfall and hit my head."

The man pushed himself off the tree, ready to move again. "I know you trespassers would like to talk all day, but it ain't gettin' any lighter. And your friend needs to get some pain medicine in him. Lucky for him I keep some around. Comes in handy when you ain't got a phone."

No phone. Lucas had been so happy to find someone, he'd forgotten what the man in the store had said about the old hermit.

No phone.

No car.

They were going back to the snake man's house, and there'd be no way to get help. No one would even know where they were. Lucas wanted to tell the old man he'd changed his mind, that he'd just stay put with Alex and George and let the rescuers find them.

But the rescuers were probably just getting started. Even if they found the message on the rock, they would never get down this far by tonight. He didn't have a choice. He had to trust the old man.

CHAPTER 21

After giving George less than a minute to rest, the old man walked over to Alex, grabbed him by the shirt, and lifted him from the ground with one hand. He bent over, wrapped an arm around the boy's legs, and tossed him over one shoulder like a sack of concrete. Alex grunted in pain from all the jostling, but he didn't protest.

Lucas couldn't believe the old man's strength. "Are you going to carry him like that the whole way?" he asked.

"I sure ain't dancin' with him." The man started off through the woods, going away from the falls Lucas had tried to descend.

"Where are you going?" Lucas asked. "I thought your house was down there somewhere." He pointed downstream, but the old man kept walking.

"I ain't gettin' past them falls with your friend here on my back," he yelled over his shoulder. "And I'm guessin' he don't want to get down the way you did. If you're comin', stay close and stop flappin' your yap. This hollow's been my backyard for seventy years. I believe I can find my way home."

Lucas and George fell in behind the old man, dropping back just enough to whisper.

"Where'd you find this guy?" asked George. "Talk about creepy."

Lucas wasn't sure George remembered the old man from Aaron's story, and he didn't see any reason to let the younger boy know who was leading them through the woods.

"Like I said, he found me. He says we're on his land. All I know is, he's the only chance we've got for getting Alex some help and getting out of here."

"Yeah, but you heard him. He doesn't even have a phone. No one's gonna know where we are."

Lucas was still worried about the same thing, but the alternative was even worse. "You want to stay out here another night?"

Before George could answer, the old man hollered back at them. "You all can either keep up, or you can keep lollygaggin' back there and end up just as lost as when I found you. But I sure ain't comin' back to get you."

With every one of the man's bouncing steps, Alex let out a feeble moan. Lucas and George gave each other one more nervous look, but they hurried after the strange old man carrying their friend.

At first the man made his own path through the thick forest. To Lucas it seemed impossible for him to know where he was going. But after some time, he saw that they were following a faint trail, no wider than a boot. To Lucas it looked like no more than a game trail. It didn't seem to lead to anything but more empty wilderness.

The old man never slowed. He had more than a hundred pounds slung over his shoulder, but Lucas still had a hard time keeping up. It didn't help that his stomach was empty, or that he'd gone more than a day now without water. Or that he was constantly stopping to wait for George. When the old man finally paused for a break and lowered Alex to the ground, Lucas plopped down, exhausted, in the middle of the path. A few seconds later, George emerged from a bend in the trail and did the same.

"Don't get too comfortable," the old man said. He wasn't breathing nearly as hard as Lucas, and he didn't even sit down to rest. "We got another half mile."

"Jeez, I need food," gasped George.

"Yeah, and that's about the hundredth time you said so since I found you," the hermit told him.

"We at least need some water," Lucas said defiantly. "Especially Alex."

"Well, unless you can figure a way to suck it out of these

trees, I'd say the nearest water's at my place. You ain't gonna die before then, are you? Let's go," the old man said, hauling Alex up onto his shoulder again and trudging off through the trees, seemingly unconcerned whether Lucas and George followed.

Soon they came to a rusted and fallen barbed-wire fence with a broad clearing on the other side. The sun had sunk below the mountains, but the light at the edge of the woods was enough to make Lucas squint after being in the dim forest all day. The clearing had probably been a farm field long ago, but now it only sprouted spiky cedars from a tangle of tall grass and wild roses. Lucas still didn't know where the old man was taking them, but they finally seemed to be leaving the wilderness.

They skirted the edge of the field, walking along the old, rotted posts of the fence for a few hundred yards. Lucas was looking at the ground, watching for half-buried strands of rusty barbed wire, when the old man finally spoke.

"Down there," he said more to the boy slung over his shoulder than the others trailing behind. The old man didn't break stride, but Lucas stopped and looked up.

A house lay below them in another field. If it was the old man's, it wasn't what he'd expected.

This house was easily more than a hundred years old, but it was clean and painted a fresh white, with bright blue shutters. Its redbrick chimney was straight and sturdy looking, and its shiny tin roof had only a few streaks of rust. Even from far away, Lucas could see neat curtains in all the windows. The house seemed totally out of place, especially considering the rough character that lived there.

Behind the house was an enormous tree, much taller than the building, its deep, green canopy spreading out more than twice its height. Away from its shade, a neatly tended vegetable garden sat surrounded by a high deer fence, and several straight rows of orchard trees lined the slope of a hill. Farther away from the house, one tiny outbuilding stood near the foot of a rock outcrop that jutted out from a green hillside like the bow of a long-buried ship. Lucas recalled that the man didn't have a bathroom, so he guessed the little building was his outhouse. It was the only part of the picture that didn't surprise him. Otherwise, nobody who saw this house could have guessed much about the character living in it.

They came up to the house from the back, below the little orchard and past the vegetable garden. From up close, the yard was even tidier. Beneath the wide, shady tree, a thick bed of acorns crunched under Lucas's feet. An oak. He saw from its massive and knotted trunk that the tree was much older than the old farmhouse, like maybe the big oak was the reason the house was there in the first place. For a second, he paused under the old tree and surveyed the little farm and its valley, thinking how nice it would be to grow up in such a place.

The four of them went up onto the back porch. Without saying a word, the man disappeared through a screen door, Alex still dangling from his shoulder. Lucas didn't want to leave his friend, but he didn't feel right just following them in. The old man sure hadn't invited them. So he and George stood on the porch, staring back out at the garden in the twilight.

That's when Lucas saw the gravestones.

"Look," he said to George.

They were no more than fifty feet from the house. From up on the hill, they'd been hidden in the shadow of the big tree. It was a family plot, maybe a dozen headstones surrounded by a low iron fence. Some of the markers looked ancient, tilted and covered in clumps of crusted moss. Most were too small or too eroded by time to make out the names and dates carved into their faces.

One, however, stood out from the rest. It was larger than the others, and it rested nearly in the center of the crowded plot. In large letters weathered smooth by the years, it was marked with the name *Morris*.

Just then a voice boomed from inside the house, making both boys jump.

"You come all the way down that mountain to spend the night outside?"

CHAPTER 22

The old man had already set Alex in a chair and propped up his bad leg in another. He had removed the crude splint and was wrapping a cloth bandage around the boy's ankle. Alex was trying hard not to make noise, but the look on his ghost-white face told Lucas how much pain he was in. While Lucas and George stood and watched, the old man made up an ice pack and wrapped it against Alex's ankle with another bandage.

When he was finished, he said, "Let's see that bite, boy."

Alex had been holding the snake-bit hand against his body, and he extended it for the old man to examine. The swelling didn't seem any worse, but it obviously pained Alex to move it.

The old man looked closely at Alex's thumb for a minute. "Looks like he just got you with one." He put two fingers to Alex's throat, which made the boy flinch. "Just checkin' your pulse. Don't get all jumpy on me." The old man waited a few seconds, counting the beats in Alex's neck. "Not racin' at all," he said. "Probably mostly a dry bite. Lucky."

"Lucky?" said Lucas. "Maybe it was one of your snakes that bit him in the first place." He figured the snake man would snap at him or maybe worse, but instead he just shook his head and laughed.

"Your busted-up friend here was mutterin' somethin' about that all the way down the mountain. Sounds like I'm gonna have to have a talk with them people over at the camp. They ain't exactly paintin' me in the best light."

"They said you put snakes out there to keep treasure hunters away."

The old man didn't respond at first, just went to the sink and refilled the ice tray he'd emptied for Alex's ice pack. He set the tray back in the freezer, and when he spoke, his voice was carrying a threatening edge.

"Look, boy," he said. "It's true I don't take kindly to trespassers, especially money-grubbin' ones. But that don't mean I like messin' with snakes." He shook his head. "Aaron told you that bullcrap, didn't he? I sure bet he did."

Lucas was surprised the hermit knew any of the counselors by name. Something told him Aaron would rather stay anonymous to the creepy old man. He kept his mouth shut while the old man retrieved a glass from a cabinet and filled it with water. When he was finished, he turned back to Lucas.

"Boy, I don't suppose you know what the name of this place is, do you? It's called Moccasin Hollow. Been called that for more'n two hundred years. 'Highland moccasin' was what them old timers used to call a copperhead. This place was so thick with 'em, they named it after the snakes— Moccasin Hollow. Now, I may look two hundred years old to you, but it sure weren't me that put all them copperheads in this hollow."

When he spoke to Alex, his voice was only a little gentler. "I'll get you something for that pain, but your bite ain't a bad one."

Alex held up his arm gingerly. It was still swollen past the wrist, and his hand was a deep red with a bluish bruise around the bite. "What do you call a bad one?" he asked weakly.

Without speaking, the old man set his boot up on a kitchen chair and slid his pant leg up to expose his calf. Above his tattered wool sock, the muscle was half gone and what remained was twisted and glossy, like the wax from a melted candle.

"Jeez!" George muttered.

He touched his own calf. "That's what a *full* load of venom can do. 'Course that was a timber rattler, and it didn't help I had to walk six miles into town for the right kind of doctorin'."

The old man set the glass of water in front of Alex and went out of the kitchen. They heard him climb the stairs, and when he returned, he had a brown prescription bottle half-full of white pills. "This is some strong stuff, and I ought not give it to you." He broke one of the pills in half with his thumb and handed it to Alex. "But I can guess how that hand's feelin'."

If Alex was afraid to take medicine from the man, he didn't show it. He swallowed it down and finished off the water in a hurry.

"That medicine will probably put you out for a while, so I'm gonna set you where you can sleep." He scooped Alex up off his chair, cradling him like a baby. Before he left the kitchen, he turned back to Lucas and George.

"You two gonna just sit there?"

They followed the old man toward the front of the house, to a bedroom off one side of the main room. He told George to click on a lamp by the door. The bedroom looked like it hadn't been used in years. Even if it had, it was too girlish to be the old man's.

White lace curtains framed a big bay window that let in the warm glow of the setting sun. A high-backed, red-velvet chair with flowers carved along the arms and legs rested in one corner. Across the room sat a small dresser and mirror with a little flowered stool set in front of it, the kind of place where a lady would put on her makeup. The bed was stark white, with lacy fringes along the bottom of the bedcover and a dark, carved headboard.

Next to the bed was a nightstand with a small lamp, its shade fringed with tiny golden tassels. On the nightstand was a single dusty book with a green cover and old-fashioned, gold lettering—*The Life and Letters of John Muir.* Lucas recognized the name from the quote above the camp office.

Without pulling back the covers, the old man laid Alex down on the bed. If he minded the bed getting dirty, he didn't show it. He pulled the tall red chair and the little stool to the side of the bed and motioned Lucas and George to sit down. "You all can set here with him a while. I suppose I'll have to get to feedin' you too." He walked back in the direction of the kitchen, grumbling.

To Lucas, the clean, white bedcover surrounding Alex made his battered friend seem even more frail, like someone lying sick in a hospital bed. "Does it hurt bad? The snakebite, I mean," he asked.

"Not as much now, but maybe I'm just getting used to it," said Alex feebly. "It still burns pretty good though. But my ankle only hurts when I move it." He perked up a little. "Hey, what's with this place? Practically a mansion, and it's just him livin' here?"

"He probably murdered everyone in it," whispered George. "I bet they're buried in the basement. Or maybe in that graveyard out back."

"I doubt it, George," Lucas whispered back. "He's mean

all right, but he's taking care of Alex, isn't he? Why would he do that if he was just going to make us disappear?"

"Who knows?" replied George, glancing back at the door in case the old man was there listening. "But the sooner we get out of here, the better. You know he doesn't have a phone? We're just as lost as we were last night. Only now, nobody even knows where to look for us."

"Well," said Lucas, "if them rescuers are any smarter than a box of rocks, they'll figure out whose hollow we went down into. I wouldn't start worryin' unless they don't show up here by morning."

Alex opened and closed his eyes slowly, looking drowsy already. "Whew, I think that medicine he gave me is already kicking in."

"Maybe he's going to knock us all out with the same medicine," said George.

"Good Lord, George," replied Lucas. "Maybe we all slept in a cave last night, and Alex here is beat. Jeez." He glanced out the cracked door toward the kitchen and lowered his voice to a whisper again. "Look, Alex, you sleep. We'll talk to him and try to find out what he's thinking. If you're still awake, we'll let you know somehow."

Alex nodded. Lucas turned off the light but left the door ajar. He and George headed back to the kitchen and the strange old man waiting there.

CHAPTER 23

The old man was at the table. A bowl filled with some kind of dark stew sat in front of him, and a pot on the back of the stove was steaming. The smell that filled the kitchen set Lucas's stomach rumbling.

"Go ahead," said the old man. He pointed with his spoon to a couple of spare bowls already set out on the counter. "Toilet's around the corner if you want to clean yourself up first."

George pushed past Lucas to the bathroom and was already back in the kitchen filling his bowl with stew before Lucas even had a chance to wash up.

When Lucas closed the bathroom door behind him, he recalled the words of the storekeeper again, about how the old man only had an outhouse. *One rumor about him that ain't true at least,* Lucas thought. He was glad to know he wouldn't have to trudge past the graveyard and up the hill to the little shack in the rocks if he needed to go in the middle of the night.

Back in the kitchen, Lucas ladled his bowl full of stew. He recognized the smell—venison stew. He doubted George had ever had any, but the younger boy was standing near the kitchen sink, hunched over his bowl and shoveling stew into his mouth like he hadn't eaten in a week. As worried as the younger boy was about the old man drugging them, he didn't seem concerned enough to refuse his food. Lucas moved his own bowl to another spot on the counter and began to eat.

"I ain't gonna bite," the old man said gruffly. He kicked the two chairs across from him so they slid out from under table. "There's cups up in that cabinet there."

Lucas found two clean glasses and passed one to George. He filled his at the sink. It was the first water he'd had in more than a day, and he drank down a whole glass then refilled it after George had done the same. The boys took their stew and water over to the table and sat down across from the old man without saying a word.

The stew was as good as it smelled, and Lucas had already eaten half a bowl before the old man spoke again.

"Your friend sleepin'?"

"He probably is by now," Lucas replied. "Had a lot rougher day than us."

"Yeah," agreed George nervously. He pushed away from

the table and wiped his mouth with the back of his hand. "Uh, do you mind if I have seconds?"

The man only shrugged and motioned with his spoon again. George headed for the pot on the stove, and the old man looked up at Lucas.

"I'll be needin' all your names," he said sternly.

Lucas and George glanced quickly at each other, and the old man saw the suspicion in their eyes.

"For when them camp people come lookin' for you, which they hopefully will by mornin'," he added grumpily. It was the first time the old man had even hinted at getting them back to Camp Kawani.

"Well," explained Lucas, "our friend's name is Alex. Alex Cruz."

"George Funderburk," answered George as he sat back down with his second bowl of stew.

The old man looked at Lucas. "And you?" he asked.

"Lucas Whitlatch, sir."

"Whiplash?"

George chuckled under his breath, and the old man shot him an icy glare. "You pokin' fun at my hearin', boy?"

George melted into his chair. "No, sir," he stammered, "it's just that I, uh, thought the same thing when I met him. You know, that Lucas's name was Whiplash."

"It's Whit*latch*, sir," interrupted Lucas. "Kind of a funny name."

He realized the old man had kept his own identity a secret, so he worked up the courage to ask.

"We don't know *your* name either. I mean, my grandma's gonna want to know who found me."

"Yeah," agreed George, "that, and we're in your house and everything."

The old man cast a wary eye across the table, like he was deciding whether or not to trust the two strangers with even his name.

"Gideon Creech," he finally said, still staring. "Ol' Giddy is what they call me in town. 'Cept that 'giddy' means crazy to them." A grin broke across his face. "'Nuttier than a squirrel turd, that Ol' Giddy' is what they'll tell you."

George chuckled again and Creech shot him a look.

"Well, thank you for helping us, Mr. Creech," offered Lucas. "And for the food and all."

Creech shrugged. "I can't have kids wanderin' off and gettin' killed on my land. A man can get into all sorts of trouble if a dead body or two turns up on his property."

The way he said it made Lucas think he was speaking from experience. He'd taken in a three lost kids, but that still didn't mean he'd have any sympathy for grown-up treasure hunters. Creech's talk of bodies made him think of the graves out back, including the one marked *Morris*. The name felt familiar.

"I thought maybe your name was Morris," Lucas said. "I saw it on one of the gravestones out there."

Creech furrowed his brow and quickly dropped his eyes back to his bowl. He took another spoonful of stew.

The old man's odd silence jarred the rest of the memory from Lucas's head. Morris was the old innkeeper from the treasure story. Lucas knew it was a sore subject with the old man, but his curiosity got the best of him.

"The counselors at the camp told us a story about a treasure around here, about some secret codes that an innkeeper kept for some explorer who disappeared out west. The innkeeper's name was Morris too."

The man's chair scraped back and he got up, acting like he hadn't heard Lucas. He took his bowl to the stove and ladled it half-full again before he spoke.

"That grave out there's the innkeeper's daughter, Annie. My grandmother with three greats. She spent the first eighteen years of her life in that inn. Wasn't too far from here," Creech said, "but it's long gone now. 'Course that treasure story is just that," he added. "A *story*. I hope them camp folks told you that part too."

"That's what they said," Lucas answered.

"Well, that don't seem to stop a lot of folks from wanderin' into my hollow to look for it." He set his bowl down in front of him and caught Lucas's eye again. "Lookin' for somethin' that wouldn't even belong to them in the first place, even if it did exist."

Lucas felt the old man's words cutting through him, and he was happy when Creech changed the subject.

"You say your name's Whitlatch?"

"Yes, sir." *Why are you asking?*

"Where you from, Lucas Whitlatch?"

"West Virginia."

Creech didn't reply, but he was paying attention, so Lucas went on.

"My town is called Indian Hole. Not really a town. More like just a road that dead-ends up against a mountain. But it's where all my kin is from, I guess."

Creech wiped the corner of his mouth with a knobby thumb. He pushed his bowl away and reached into his pocket, drawing out a pipe. From the same pocket, he retrieved a pouch of tobacco.

"How'd you come to be in that camp?" he asked.

"What do you mean, sir?" If Creech knew what the camp was about, he already knew why Lucas was there.

"I *mean*, did you lose your pa or your ma?"

"My pa, Mr. Creech."

"He a soldier?" Creech asked, packing tobacco into the bowl of his pipe.

"Yes, sir," replied Lucas, a little surprised. "How did you know?"

"Didn't," Creech said. "Just a lucky guess. Or more like unlucky for your pa, I reckon."

"I reckon too." Lucas figured it was the closest thing to sympathy he'd get from the crusty old hermit.

Creech struck a match and lit his pipe, sucking the flame down onto the tobacco. Once it was lit, a stream of blue smoke curled through the bristly white hair surrounding his lips. The smoke enveloped him, and he seemed to drift off in a daze, like he was thinking on something from another time.

George caught Lucas's eye and arched his eyebrows, a look that said, *Now what?*

Lucas pushed his chair back. "Thanks for the stew, Mr. Creech." He took his bowl and spoon to the sink and rinsed them. George took his cue and did the same.

Creech stayed at the table, his pipe smoke drifting up into an old brass light hanging above him. Even when he spoke, he still had a faraway look in his eyes.

"I'm goin' to check on your friend's snakebite one more time. There's another room across from him. I expect we'll have company by first light."

Lucas figured it was Gideon Creech's way of saying good night.

CHAPTER 24

They found the bedroom down the hall and a lamp just inside. Compared to the fancy room where Alex was sleeping, this room was plain. Two narrow beds with simple, square headboards and a small dresser were pushed against the walls. On top of the dresser next to the lamp lay a dusty, old-fashioned baseball mitt that reminded Lucas of the players in baggy uniforms and tiny caps he'd seen in old pictures. The walls were empty except for a puny rack of deer antlers and a couple hooks that held an antique-looking BB gun. Lucas wondered if this had been Creech's room when he was a boy. Like the bedroom across the parlor, it looked as if decades had passed since anyone had slept in it.

"Better than a cave in the woods," he whispered to George.

"Maybe," replied George, his eyes wide to let Lucas know he still saw Creech as a threat.

Lucas sat down on the bed closest to the door and slipped

off his boots. The room was musty and warm, so he got up and pried open the only window, pausing to breathe in the cool night air. Investigating another door, he found that it led out to a small porch at the corner of the house. He was exhausted, but the night outside felt better than the stuffy house, so he turned out the bedroom light to keep from attracting bugs and started out the door.

George had already settled into his bed. "What are you doing?" he asked in a panicked whisper.

"I can't breathe in here," he said. "Don't worry, I won't be out here long." He left the door open a crack on his way out.

He swatted the dust and old spiderwebs off a rusty chair and sat down. The crickets and katydids were roaring compared to the quiet of the old farmhouse, and fireflies flickered against the dark wall of the trees edging the meadow around the house. Above, in the last of the twilight, bats dove and spiraled, hunting bugs attracted to the dim light from the house. A breeze carried the damp scent of freshly mowed hay. In the distant valley west, the soft lights of other farms sparkled, and the sight of them reminded Lucas of how far he was from Indian Hole. Before long, his eyelids drooped and he nodded off to sleep.

When he woke, there were more stars, and the moon had risen higher. He had slept for an hour, maybe longer. Groggily, he pulled himself to his feet and rolled his head on his shoulders to loosen the stiffness in his neck. The door to the bedroom was still cracked, and he stepped back inside. The room had cooled some, and George was snoring softly. Quietly, Lucas sat down on his bed, stripped off his dirty shirt, and lay back on his pillow.

He had just drifted off again when the floor outside his door creaked.

Careful not to stir the covers, Lucas lifted his head enough to see the shadow of a tall figure cast by the moonlight streaming into his room from the parlor.

Creech was just outside the door, looking in and listening.

Then the faintest of footsteps crossed the parlor, moving away. He heard a metallic click, and a soft-green light filled the crack of the bedroom door.

Lucas slowly swung his legs to the floor and crept silently to the doorway, keeping his face back in the shadows as he peered out.

The light came from a green-shaded lamp on top of a large, rolltop desk. Creech was hunched over the desk, the side of his wrinkled face glowing in the lamplight as he quietly worked a key into the lock for the desk top. He was moving slowly, glancing back at the bedrooms every so often. Whatever he was doing, he was trying hard to keep it a secret.

Creech slid the desk top up inch by inch, then reached in with both hands to remove a small box. Its worn wood had a soft, antique glow, and a small, black padlock was hooked to the front. Creech left the top of the desk up and clicked off the lamp. He held the box closely to his chest with one hand and turned to go back upstairs. At Lucas's door, he stopped again.

For a moment, he stared directly into the shadows where Lucas was hidden. But then the old man was out of sight, his footsteps ascending the creaky staircase.

Lucas crept closer to his door, enough to stick his head out and peek up the stairs. There was no sign of Creech, not even a light from upstairs.

Scared as he was, Lucas couldn't help wondering what else was hidden inside the old desk. Stepping as lightly as he could, he crept across the moonlit parlor.

He didn't dare turn on the light, but even without it, he could make out the dusty surface of the desk. There was a dark rectangular imprint left behind by the old box Creech had just removed, as if the box had been there a long time.

A book lay next to the outline of the missing box. It was small and thin with a handwritten title scrawled on a primitive cover made from some kind of smooth bark and bound with a tattered red ribbon. The book looked like something out of a museum.

Without disturbing the dust, Lucas gingerly picked up the book and moved over to a moonlit window to read the title.

Blue Ridge Verses. By Annie Morris.

A book by the old man's ancestor, the same one buried outside.

Lucas opened the book to the first page and saw that the handwritten words were a poem titled *Leaves*.

Turning more pages, he found that each held a different poem, all in the same fancy cursive. The edges of each page were brown and brittle, and he had to be careful not to tear them from the ribbon holding them between the covers.

He noted a few of the poems' titles and read some of their first lines. Most had to do with the mountains or the forest, though a couple were more like love poems. Lucas imagined a teenaged girl growing up in the shadow of the mountains, wandering the same waterfall-laced hollows and rocky peaks the three of them had struggled through the last two days.

But their experience had been an ordeal. Annie Morris's words described her mountain world as a paradise—just like Lucas's was to him.

Suddenly the ceiling creaked, and the sound of footsteps crossed toward the top of the stairs.

Creech was coming back.

Lucas closed the book and moved quickly away from the window. He was still holding it delicately, trying not to disturb the dust on its cover, and when he stepped toward the desk, he lost his grip. The book fell from his hands. Its pages fluttered, and Lucas knew Creech would hear it hit the floor.

He shot his hand out blindly, barely snagging the old book by one cover.

Frantically, Lucas placed the book back in its spot on the desk. By now, Creech was at the top of the stairs, where he'd surely see Lucas run for the bedroom. Lucas looked around the parlor in a panic. He scurried to the one corner that lay in the shadows and put his back to the wall just as Creech's legs appeared on the staircase.

Creech crept down the stairs with the old box in his hand. He glanced once at Lucas's room, then walked silently back to the desk. For a terrifying moment, Lucas expected him to turn on the lamp again. Instead, he placed the box next to the book and began to close the desk.

Then Creech stopped.

He leaned in closer and touched the book's cover. Quietly, he picked it up and moved to stand by the same moonlit window where Lucas had been just moments before.

Lucas's heart hammered in his chest as Creech examined the book. Surely, he'd left fingerprints or knocked the dust off when he'd caught it. Creech would know he'd held it just minutes ago. And the old man would find him, hiding like a thief.

But Creech moved out of the light and set the book back in place. He closed the desk and locked it, not quite as concerned about keeping quiet now. He dropped the desk key in his shirt pocket and started for the stairs.

When he reached the door to Lucas's room, he stopped to look in again.

Across the parlor in the shadows, Lucas could see George's bed illuminated by the moonlight from the parlor, but his own empty bed was out of sight, hidden in darkness behind the door. He watched as Creech lightly placed his hand on the door and began to slowly push it open, trying to peer deeper inside. What would Creech do to him when he caught him snooping around?

Just then, George's rhythmic snoring erupted into a single mighty snort that seemed to rattle the entire house.

Creech and Lucas both nearly jumped out of their skin.

It took Creech a few seconds to recover from the scare, but George's snoring seemed to satisfy him that both boys were asleep, and he backed away from the door. Casting a final glance toward the desk, the old man disappeared up the dim staircase.

Lucas let out his breath, but he waited until Creech's steps crossed the ceiling above him before tiptoeing back across the parlor. As he passed the old desk, the curtains fluttered and the breeze blew something bright across the floor at his feet.

A piece of paper.

Lucas reached for it, and when he touched its brittle edges, he knew what it was.

One of the poems. It had come loose when he'd dropped the book.

He started to slip it under the locked top of the desk but stopped. If the old man opened the desk in the morning, he'd know someone had been in it. There was no way he could get the page back into the book, not without telling Creech, and he wasn't about to do that. Not without being a long way from Moccasin Hollow first.

Careful not to tear the paper, Lucas folded the page and put it delicately into his pocket. He slipped back into the bedroom without moving the door and climbed into bed. After thinking on it for a few minutes, he decided he'd explain the page to Maggie and hope she wasn't too afraid to return it to Moccasin Hollow for him.

Once Lucas's heart finally stopped racing, it didn't take long for his exhausted body to give in. He fell asleep wondering about the box in the desk and why the old man was so bent on sneaking it to his room in the middle of the night.

CHAPTER 25

The room was already bright when Lucas woke.

George was watching him. "Jeez, Lucas, I didn't think you were ever going to wake up. He's cooking breakfast in there, but you gotta go in with me."

Lucas started to tell George about Creech's mysterious retrieval of the old box, but a faint thumping noise interrupted him. George noticed him listening, and they both deciphered the noise at the same time.

Helicopter. Getting closer.

It sounded like it was coming down the side of the mountain straight toward Creech's farmhouse.

Lucas threw back the covers, and both boys dashed out into the parlor and through the kitchen, following the roar of the chopper out onto the back porch. Creech was already there, waving his arms over his head to signal the pilot, though he didn't need to. The blue-and-white helicopter hovered down over the massive oak tree in the backyard. "Virginia State Police" was painted in large blue letters beneath the pilot's window. The downdraft from the whirling blades sent a shower of leaves and grass swirling around the backyard. Over the noise of the chopper, Lucas heard Creech cursing.

Suddenly a voice boomed down at them. "If you are Alex Cruz, George Funderburk, or Lucas Whitlatch, cross your arms above your head!"

Lucas immediately signaled the helicopter, and George followed his lead.

"If the third boy is with you, make the same signal!" Lucas and George both crossed their arms again.

The loudspeaker blared again. "If any of you needs immediate medical attention, make the same signal!"

This time Lucas wasn't sure. He hadn't even seen Alex this morning. The old man shook his head, but Lucas figured Creech just didn't want the helicopter landing in the middle of his backyard and shredding his garden to pieces. How long would it take for help to come for Alex if the helicopter didn't take them out now?

Just then the screen door slammed behind them, and a hand came down on Lucas's shoulder, using him for support. It was Alex. He was leaning on a wooden crutch, but he was smiling.

He shouted over the racket of the whirling blades. "I don't need a police helicopter for a stupid busted ankle!"

Lucas yelled back, "What about your snakebite?"

Alex held up his hand. It was still swollen and the thumb was purplish, but no worse than the night before.

"But don't you want to ride out of here in a helicopter?" George asked.

"We're in enough trouble already!" Alex yelled back. "We don't need to make it worse!"

Creech nodded in agreement, and Lucas wondered if there was some other reason he wanted to keep the Virginia State Police out of Moccasin Hollow.

The pilots didn't wait any longer for their reply. "Stay at this location! Help will arrive soon!" The helicopter gained altitude, tilted forward, and glided over the house and into the valley.

Creech looked at Alex. "Looks like somebody else gets to carry you today," he snorted. "I'd like to see the looks on their faces when they find out I ain't got no driveway." He went back inside and the boys followed him, Alex hobbling with one arm over Lucas's shoulder.

Once inside, Alex sat down heavily at the kitchen table and propped his foot up in another chair. Creech came to rest in the chair next to him. "Let's see that bite, boy."

Alex laid his arm on the table, wincing only a little when he did. The old man took his hand gently and looked closely at the bitten thumb. "Like I said, mostly a dry one. Won't be able to use it all the way for a while, but I guess you get to keep your hand after all."

Alex smiled brightly for the first time in two days. "I don't think I'll be alive long enough to worry about my hand if I don't get some food in me. I dreamed about food all night."

Creech got up and pulled an old crock from the refrigerator. He retrieved a dozen eggs and a slab of bacon wrapped in brown paper. "Can't have them gossipy fools in town thinking Ol' Giddy tried to starve you to death too."

After he fixed the breakfast, Creech disappeared upstairs, but the three boys spent nearly an hour at the table. Alex ate so much that even George warned him to slow down. By the time Lucas took his dishes to the sink, Alex had eaten a bowl of the leftover stew, half a dozen eggs, and nearly a dozen thick strips of bacon.

All of a sudden, they heard a shout from the field at the front of the house. "Mr. Creech? You up there? I hear you've been keeping some of our campers for us."

It was Maggie.

The old man came down the stairs yelling.

"And I hear you and that brother of yours can't keep track of the young 'uns you got over there. They're endin' up on my property like dogs off a busted chain."

They heard footsteps on the porch and the shuffle of other people entering the parlor. Lucas figured it was a bigger crowd than the old man had seen in a long time. Creech entered the kitchen first, and Maggie was close behind, with two paramedics on her heels. One carried a folded-up stretcher, and the other lugged a big orange case. Both were sweating heavily and breathing hard.

Maggie started to speak but stopped when she saw Alex's swollen hand and bandaged ankle. "I thought you told the chopper you didn't need first aid. What did you do to yourself?"

Alex held up his hand. "Sorry, Maggie. I got bit by a copperhead. Knocked me off a rock too, and I think my ankle's busted. He glanced at the old man. "Mr. Creech here found us and got me back here. Not sure how, but he did."

Lucas interrupted. "It's true, Maggie. He took care of Alex's bite. Carried him down the mountain on his back too."

"And speakin' of snakes," Creech interrupted, "you best tell your brother to stop with all his crazy-snake-man business, or he's gonna get a visit from me. Probably givin' them campers nightmares."

One of the paramedics pushed his way around the table and started examining Alex's hand. The other one was already preparing a syringe. "We'll give you something for the pain," he said.

"I gave him somethin' last night, and he didn't even need nothin' this morning." Creech snickered. "Stop babyin' him. His bite ain't bad."

"I'll need to see what you gave him, Mr. Creech," insisted the paramedic who was examining Alex's bite.

"It's right there on the counter. Same stuff you so-called *professionals* use."

"These men are here to help," Maggie said sternly. "And they've got to stretcher Alex a half mile back to the car all because *someone* doesn't believe in having a driveway."

It was obvious that Maggie and Creech weren't tangling for the first time. But Creech didn't seem to mind Maggie standing up to him. In fact, he ignored her and grinned at the paramedics. "And he ain't exactly light as a feather," he chuckled, enjoying himself.

Maggie shook her head at the old man's rudeness and turned back to the boys. "How exactly did you three get so lost?"

Lucas didn't hesitate. "It was my fault. I talked Alex and George into exploring a cave we saw. It was up in the Preacher Rocks."

"A cave?" asked Maggie incredulously. "You mean like the kind we said you could get killed in?"

"I thought maybe it would be a good hiding place for…" He dropped his head. He felt safe calling himself a treasure hunter in front of Creech now, but that didn't help the embarrassment.

"The treasure? Oh man." She sighed. "You have *got* to be

kidding." She sounded like she might explode, but Creech beat her to it.

He slammed his hand down on the table, making everyone in the crowded kitchen jump. But the anger wasn't directed at Lucas. He was glaring at Maggie.

"And that's *exactly* why you and that brother of yours ought to be keeping your traps shut about the treasure!"

"Just wait a minute!" she snapped back. "We ran into a couple of treasure hunters on a hike. Right up from the camp. The kids all wanted to know what a couple of strange men were doing digging in our woods. What were we suppose to tell them?"

The old man groaned. "What do you think a bunch of kids are gonna do if you tell 'em there's millions of dollars buried around here? They're kids, ain't they?"

"We told them it's just a story." She glared at her three campers. "Only *three* of them didn't listen so well."

One of the paramedics interrupted. "Miss Cates, we still need to get this one to the hospital. His bite looks okay, but his ankle's in bad shape. And it's going to take a while getting him back down that trail."

"You're right," Maggie agreed. Her tone softened, and she walked over to the old man. "I suppose we do owe you a big thank-you, even if you are a cantankerous old hermit."

She stuck out her hand as if to shake, but when he

reluctantly reached out, she surprised him with a quick kiss on the cheek. Lucas and George looked at each other, and even the paramedics looked shocked.

Creech turned bright red and bristled at the attention. "I suppose I don't get no reimbursement, do I? These boys nearly ate me out of house and home. I'll need to make an extra trip into town now just to restock."

One of the paramedics encased Alex's lower leg in an inflatable splint, and they hefted him onto the stretcher. Lucas and George followed as they carried him out onto the front porch, and Creech walked out behind Maggie.

At the bottom of the stairs, Lucas turned back to Creech. He wanted to thank the old man, but Creech simply nodded at him before he got the chance. When Lucas turned to head down the hill, the old man was still standing at his door with Maggie.

Lucas caught up to George and the paramedics and walked beside his friend on the stretcher. Alex was strapped down so he couldn't fall off.

"Talk about embarrassing," he mumbled glumly.

They walked downhill through Creech's front yard, along a well-worn trail to where the woods began. Lucas saw that the path was really a set of old, overgrown wheel ruts.

"Looks like somebody had a driveway here once," commented one of the paramedics.

"Tracks are too narrow for a car," replied the other from the front of the stretcher. "Maybe wagons, but a *long* time ago." He stopped and looked back up at the house. "Think we ought to wait for her?" he asked his partner.

Maggie was still on the front porch talking with the old man. Creech waved his hands in front of her, like he was still angry about something and letting her know. Lucas figured they were still arguing about her campers getting lost or maybe negotiating what the camp would owe him for his troubles.

They watched as Creech went back into the house. He returned with a piece of paper and shoved it into her hands. As she read it, Creech kept talking and pointing toward them. Then Maggie nodded once and handed the paper back to Creech.

"Probably a bill for all the food you three ate," joked one of the paramedics.

"Or maybe he's charging you for staying overnight," said the other. "C'mon, Alex here has a date with a doctor."

CHAPTER 26

Maggie caught up just as they emerged from the forest at the edge of a gravel road. From there, Creech's house was well-hidden from sight and even the spot on the road felt like the middle of nowhere. An orange-and-white ambulance sat on the far shoulder. Behind it was a green pickup with the Camp Kawani logo on the door.

Lucas and George started to follow their friend's stretcher, but Maggie stopped them.

"Sorry, guys," she said softly. "You're going to have to say good-bye to Alex here."

"Can't we go to the hospital with him?" pleaded George.

"Especially not you, George. Your father wants you back at the camp." She looked at her watch. "He got off a plane in Baltimore about an hour ago. He said he'd be down here by this evening."

"*My* dad? Right," George grunted. "He's in California for the week."

Maggie put her hand on his shoulder. "George, he was worried to death. As soon as he found out you were lost, he probably called us a dozen times. He caught a red-eye flight last night. We told him to get a little sleep before he drove down from Maryland, but he insisted on seeing you safe— with his own eyes."

George didn't reply, but his expression said he still didn't believe her.

"What about me?" Lucas asked. "I could ride in the ambulance with him."

"Not according to your grandmother, Lucas," Maggie replied. "We've been in touch with her too, and she wants you back with the other campers, ASAP. Besides, how would we get you back to camp if I let you go to the hospital?"

By now, the paramedics were gently setting Alex onto a bigger stretcher, one with wheels that they could load into the ambulance.

"What about Alex?" George asked. "Will he get to come back to the camp?"

"Not with his injuries," explained Maggie. "He'll probably spend today in the hospital, maybe tonight depending on his ankle. His father is driving down to see him after work, maybe sooner once we tell him Alex got hurt. Whenever he gets released from the hospital, he's going straight home."

Home. The word reminded Lucas how soon his Camp

Kawani week would be over.

He left George with Maggie and walked up to the side of Alex's stretcher. The paramedics were packing their equipment, leaving the two boys alone.

"You coming to the hospital?" Alex asked.

"Maggie says we can't. She's already got my grandma all fired up about me gettin' back."

"I guess I'll check you back at the camp, then," Alex said hopefully.

Lucas hated to tell him. "Your father's coming down by tonight. He's taking you home from there."

Alex only shook his head. His ankle was still trussed up in the inflatable splint, and he could barely open the fingers on his swollen, snake-bitten hand. It wasn't like he could protest.

"Well, then I guess I'll see you around, Luke Whiplash."

"Yeah, take it easy…Mexican," Lucas replied, but both boys barely cracked a smile. Lucas knew the chances of ever seeing Alex again were pretty slim, and he knew Alex figured the same.

The paramedics were hanging back, waiting for them to finish. Finally one of them interrupted.

"All right, guys, we've got to get back to town. Never know when we might have another customer." As they wheeled Alex's stretcher up to the back of the ambulance, George came up to his side too.

"Check you later, Alex," he said, and Lucas saw that the younger boy was trying not to choke up.

Alex smiled. "Go bust another Thunder Butt on 'em, George."

"Count on it," replied George.

The paramedics hefted Alex into the back of the ambulance and shut the doors. When Lucas turned back, Maggie was already waiting in the camp pickup, and he and George climbed in.

She pulled the truck onto the road and wheeled it around in a U-turn. "I'll give you both his email address when we get back to camp. You guys can stay in touch that way."

Lucas didn't want to tell her that his grandparents didn't own a computer. The only ones he got to use were the ones at school, and that was mostly just for school stuff. He thought about maybe asking Maggie for Alex's phone number, but the idea of calling him out of the blue from Indian Hole, or wherever he ended up once there was no Indian Hole, already seemed strange. What could he possibly have to talk about with someone from DC? The only thing he and Alex had in common was the camp and getting lost. And even that adventure was going to fade away fast once they went back to their own lives.

Yep. He'd probably never even talk to Alex again.

They drove in silence for a few miles until they crossed a

narrow concrete bridge over a shallow creek, coming to a stop at a crossroads where the gravel road met pavement. A sign in front of them pointed west to town. Next to the sign was a gray historical marker, something about a church named St. Mary's. Where the church had once stood, there was now only an abandoned gas station, its rusty pumps barely visible through a tangle of blackberry vines.

Alex's ambulance pulled up alongside them, blocking the view. Maggie honked her horn and the driver waved. Then he turned the ambulance, and Alex, west toward town.

Maggie waited for a truck to lumber past the intersection, heading for the gap through the mountains. On Lucas's side of the road was a wooden stand where an old woman was selling jars of honey. The honey jars sat out by the roadside, lined up atop a sagging board suspended between two short logs. The morning sun lit up the jars from the behind, making the honey glow like liquid gold.

Lucas thought once more of the treasure. *Like Creech said, it's just a story. No one will ever find it.*

CHAPTER 27

Lucas and George rode silently beside Maggie for a long time. The trip back to Camp Kawani seemed like it was taking forever, and the miles made Lucas realize how lost they'd really been. Maggie had been mostly quiet, and Lucas figured she was still more than a little angry with them for running off. He wondered what punishment awaited them back at camp.

Finally Maggie broke the silence. "Just so you know, the search-and-rescue crew found your packs down in the brush. Below the ledge where your group had lunch."

"What?" snapped Lucas. "We left 'em up on in the rocks, so we could find the trail."

Then it hit him, what Maggie was trying to tell them.

He looked at George and said, "Zack."

"Are you kidding?" said George. "This was all because of him?"

"Uh, don't forget who wandered off in the first place," Maggie reminded him. "But yeah, I guess you can thank him for the worst of your little adventure. The rescue crew said the packs were banged up, like someone had just heaved them off the ledge. When they found the first one, they thought maybe one of you had fallen. But later, a couple of the other boys said Zack hung back when Aaron and Rooster weren't looking. One even saw him knocking down cairns when he was catching back up. They didn't say anything to Aaron at first because they were scared of Zack. Either way, I guess he was pretty determined to help you get lost."

"What a butthead," muttered George.

"Yeah," agreed Lucas, "but why didn't Aaron just come back for us when we didn't catch up?"

Maggie grimaced. "Believe me, Aaron was really kicking himself. He's been leading that trip for years and never lost a camper. But when he yelled back to find out if you guys had caught up, Zack told him you were just up the trail. Unfortunately, Aaron believed him, and nobody ever turned around to see for themselves. By the time Aaron figured it out, that lightning was closing in, and he couldn't go back up on the ridge."

"So where's Zack now?" Lucas asked, hoping he'd get one last chance to take a swing at him.

"Oh, that was definitely the final straw. After that and the trouble on the zip line, we figured he needed to be home. His dad's driver is supposed to pick him up this morning."

Lucas glanced at George and saw he was thinking the same vengeful thoughts. Without Alex, he doubted George would be good for much against Zack, but he'd take all the help he could get.

Maggie sensed them simmering. "Look, guys, I know what Zack did was idiotic and dangerous—and just plain mean. But put yourself in his shoes…"

"I couldn't afford his shoes," said George.

"You know what I'm saying," Maggie said. "He just went through the same crisis you two did. His mother died, just like yours, George. Just like your father, Lucas. You both know what that was like. Even good kids can react to something like that in bad ways. To be honest, I wish we could have helped him more."

George wasn't buying it at all. "If Zack's a good kid, then I must be Jesus or something."

But Lucas recalled some of the things he'd done at camp himself, things that he never would have risked before his pa died. Like going after Zack, right in front of the counselors. Or the whole plot to embarrass him on the zip line, even if it meant fighting with him, maybe even getting kicked out of the camp. And sneaking away to the cave. Even the way he talked to Creech in the store and up in the hollow, and sneaked around his house in the middle of the night. He'd done those things because he just didn't care what happened.

Or what anyone thought of him.

He'd never been like that before the accident. It spooked him, thinking he could become a different person so quickly. Suddenly he didn't want to think about Zack anymore.

"So how come you know Mr. Creech so well?" George asked. "I thought he was supposed to be some kind of scary, old hermit. And you even kissed him."

"Oh, he's definitely a hermit," she replied with a smile. "But not too scary to me. We actually go way back. I even help him out every once in a while. I mean, we *are* neighbors in a way. It's just not something he wants me to spread around. In fact, that was the first time I've ever been up to his place with anybody but Aaron."

"In town they say he's crazy," said Lucas.

"So you heard about him in town, huh?" She shook her head and sighed. "I can only imagine."

Lucas shrugged. "He doesn't seem crazy to me." He pictured Creech stalking around the house in the dark. *Maybe not crazy but a little creepy.*

"He's not. He just wants everyone to *think* he is. Crazy and mean. If you spent the night with him, you probably got the whole act. And believe me, it's just an act."

"Why?" George asked.

"Oh," she sighed, "just to keep everyone away, I guess." She sounded like she was tired of the old man's act herself.

"He wants to be left alone. He likes it that way. Says all he needs is his old house in Moccasin Hollow to make him happy. And you know, I believe him. It's like a sanctuary to him, the quiet up there, in the forest and up on the mountain— and his creek and his orchard."

Lucas knew exactly what she meant. *But at least the old man gets to keep his mountain.*

Maggie maneuvered the truck around a section of broken road, smiling and shaking her head, like she knew something else about Creech. But she also seemed a little sad when she talked about the old man.

"He figures if he acts like a mean old coot, no one will ever bother him. Especially treasure hunters. They're always wanting to get on his property."

"Is that because he's related to the old innkeeper?" Lucas probed.

She kept her eyes on the road, but he saw her surprise. "How would you know that?" she asked.

"It was on a gravestone up there. I just asked him. He said Morris was like his great-great-great grandfather."

"One more 'great' actually. And I'm surprised he talked about it with you. That legend is a real sore subject with him."

"Do you really think it's just a legend?" Lucas asked her.

"I guess no one knows for sure. But if Mr. Creech knew

anything about it, he'd be the last one to say. He doesn't have much use for money, and he doesn't care for greedy people, especially the trespassing kind."

"But how does he know that everyone who wants the treasure is just greedy?" Lucas asked. "Maybe someone would do something good with it, something that needs to be done."

Maggie turned to him. "What would you do with it, Lucas?"

He wasn't about to tell her about his mountain. "I don't know. I just know not everybody with money has to be greedy about it."

"You mean like Zack?" George muttered.

A few minutes later, the pickup crunched to a stop in front of the office. Inside, they found Aaron at a computer behind the front desk. Maggie walked up and tossed her pack onto the counter.

"Treasure hunting," she said to her brother. "They saw a cave up in the Preacher Rocks and just *had* to check it out."

"What did I *tell* you?" Aaron said angrily. "That's *exactly* why we don't tell the story to the campers. All it takes is one kid to wander off and get hurt, and we're shut down for good."

"Well, Alex accomplished the getting hurt part—snakebite and probably a broken ankle," she reported. "In fact, I'm going to the hospital right now. Walk with me out to the truck. We need to talk."

Maggie held the door open, and Aaron came out from behind the desk. Before she left, she grabbed another pack leaning against the wall and slung one strap over her shoulder. It was Alex's.

The other two packs were there too, scuffed up some, but Lucas was relieved to see the patch across the back of his, his pa's name, still intact. He and George shouldered the packs and headed outside, where Maggie and Aaron were leaning against the camp's truck, talking quietly.

It wasn't until he and George turned out of the little parking lot onto the loop road that they saw the big luxury car parked behind Cabin Four. The same driver from the weekend before was loading Zack's gear into the trunk.

Lucas and George stopped in their tracks for a second before Lucas said, "C'mon," and started walking. "Let me do the talking," he added.

They were ten feet from the cabin when Zack came out the back and saw them. Lucas expected him to laugh at them and make some snarky comment, like something about what the cat dragged in. Lucas was ready to drop his pack and charge him when he did.

But instead, Zack went straight to the car and opened the passenger door. He sat down heavily, slammed the door, and buried his face in his hands. Lucas stopped beside Zack's window and stared in through the tinted glass. He couldn't be sure, but he thought the boy was crying. George saw it too and gave Lucas a wide-eyed shrug. There was nothing they could say even if they wanted to. They turned to go inside, but the driver's voice caught them.

"You the kids who got lost?"

"With a lot of help from him, yeah," Lucas said.

"That's what I heard. Look, it probably doesn't mean much after what you went through, but the kid is pretty sorry for it. He just doesn't have the backbone right now to tell you himself."

Lucas didn't doubt it. Not anymore. But somehow he didn't think that's what the tears were all about. He knew that in a day he'd be in the exact same shoes as Zack, going home to a different world, one that was missing the most important person in his life. And no amount of money would change that.

CHAPTER 28

Inside the cabin, Alex's bunk was bare, the mattress already stripped. The sight of it reminded Lucas that he'd probably never see his new friend again. They dropped their packs on the floor, and Lucas collapsed onto his bunk. He didn't care what George did. He only wanted sleep, and it came almost as soon as he shut his eyes.

Lucas dreamed of a deep forest cut by a tiny stream. Below each little rapid, the water settled into a clear pool where thousands of tiny trout hovered. An old man came through the trees, a faceless stranger who became Gideon Creech. He leaned his shotgun against a tree and waded into the creek, morphing into a panther as he touched the water. The panther slunk through the pools, scooping out the trout and tossing them up onto the mossy rocks along the creek. When each little fish flopped onto the rocks, it became a shiny nugget of gold.

In the dream, Lucas scrambled to catch them, but each time he lunged for one, it morphed back into a slippery trout and wriggled out of his grasp. Finally he waded into the pool himself, but before he could capture a fish of his own, he awoke to sound of their screen door slamming.

"Sorry, Lucas," whispered George sheepishly. "I was trying to be quiet."

"George," Lucas replied groggily. "Where'd you go?"

"Lunch, man, you missed it. It's like we're some kind of celebrities or something for getting lost."

"Great. What time is it?" asked Lucas, propping himself on an elbow. He wasn't even sure what day it was anymore.

George glanced at his oversized watch and pushed a button. "Five after two," he answered. "They said your grandma was up at the office a little while ago. I guess she checked in on you. Twice. But you were dead asleep both times. Guess she decided to let you sleep. They told me to tell you they got her a hotel room in town, and she'd be here at the pickup time tomorrow morning."

Lucas was sorry he'd missed his grandma, especially with so much to tell her. But now that he remembered he was down to his last afternoon at camp, he didn't want to waste it.

George was thinking the same thing. "I don't know about you, but I'm heading out to the lake. They've got the zip line going again, and I never did get a real turn at it, thanks to

Zack. You think he was really sorry?"

"Yeah, I do," Lucas replied, still wishing he'd at least heard the words from Zack himself.

"You coming?"

Lucas realized he was still wearing his jeans from the past three days, and they were filthy. He sat up on the edge of the bunk. "Yeah, but I gotta put on something I can swim in. I'll meet you at the top of the zip line."

"No problem," said George, pulling off his shirt and grabbing a towel. "Just follow the sound of my screaming fans."

Lucas watched him bound out onto the porch and down the steps, his pale belly jiggling. He got up from the bunk, riffled through his extra clothes stacked in the closet, and found a pair of shorts.

Out of habit, he emptied the pockets of his jeans before taking them off. In one, he felt the crunch of paper, and it took him a second to remember he still had the page from the old poetry book. He pulled it out gently, and began carefully smoothing out the folds. He figured he'd tell Maggie about it tonight. The way she'd handled Creech this morning, at least she wouldn't be afraid to take it back to him.

He was just about to toss the page on his bunk when he saw the numbers.

Even in the moonlight streaming into Creech's parlor, he hadn't seen them. But now, in the daylight, they were there.

Tiny numbers scrawled above every line of Annie Morris's handwritten words.

He read the poem's title—"Heaven"—and studied her handwriting. The numbers above the words were definitely in someone else's hand, not Annie's. Lucas counted ten words between each numbered one.

340
HEAVEN IS HERE 'NEATH THE MOUNTAIN WALLS,
350
IN THE SONG OF THE WIND AND THE WATERFALLS,

IN THE WATCHFUL STARS THAT BLANKET THE NIGHT
360
AND THE MUSIC OF BIRDS BEFORE THE DAWN LIGHT.

370
HEAVEN IS HERE IN OUR MOUNTAIN KEEP,
380
IN THE SILENCE AND DIM OF THE FOREST DEEP.
390
FROM THE CHESTNUT TALL AS THE MIGHTIEST MAST,
400
TO THE LAUREL FLOWERS IN THE SHADOW IT CASTS.

HEAVEN IS HERE ON THESE MOUNTAINS HIGH,
410
IN ANCIENT STONE CASTLES THAT CHALLENGE THE SKY,
420
IN THE THUNDER AND FLASH THAT RING FROM THEIR FIGHT
430
AND THE MEADOWS MADE GOLD BY THE DAY'S FINAL LIGHT.

Someone had used the book to make a code. Or someone else had used it to try and break one. Had Creech tried to break the codes using his ancestor's book?

Maggie's words from the other night, when she'd told the treasure story, came back to him: *So rare that maybe there's only one in the whole world.*

She'd said the key to Beale's other ciphers might be something so rare, there was only one ever written. *Something small and simple.* Something like a little book of poems.

There couldn't be another copy. And Annie Morris grew up in the same inn where Beale had stayed for two winters.

Frantically, Lucas fished the paper bag from the market out of the little trash can next to his bunk. Inside he found the crumpled brochure his grandma had put in with his toothpaste. The clerk had said the codes were inside, and when Lucas opened the brochure, he saw all three ciphers. They were long lists of numbers, each with its own title.

Cipher Number One: The Location of the Vault.

Cipher Number Two: The Contents of the Vault.

This one had the same translation Maggie had read to them at the campfire, the one using the Declaration of Independence.

Cipher Number Three: Names and Residences.

Desperately, Lucas dug through his daypack for something to write with and came up with a stubby pencil. Outside, the shouts from the lake told him the fun on the zip line had started. He'd have to miss it.

With the pencil, he circled all the numbers in the first cipher between 335 and 435, the range of the words in the single poem he had. In the cipher, the numbers ranged from single digits to the high hundreds. If the book of poems really was the key, he had only a small part. *Better than nothing.*

He went back through Beale's list of numbers twice to make sure he hadn't missed any. When he was done, he paused to stare at the circled numbers in the first cipher, wondering if his little poem would be enough to turn any of them into words.

He needed paper.

He'd removed his school notebooks from his daypack before the trip, so he began rummaging through George's backpack. Buried in one of the side pockets, carefully sealed in a plastic bag, he found his roommate's cherished roll of toilet paper. Only about a third of the roll was left, but he wouldn't need much. He unrolled a strip of the paper and began making notes.

Some of the circled numbers stood alone in the key. He ignored these. Single, random letters wouldn't help him.

Others were in pairs or threes. At first these only produced hopeless pairs of consonants like "L-N" or "W-T." But one string of three numbers formed "E-A-S," and Lucas wondered if this was the beginning of "EAST," the kind of word you'd see in the directions to a buried treasure.

There were only a few places in the codes where more than three numbers in a row fell within the range of the numbers in his poem. After a few of the shorter strings, he skipped to these.

The first that he tried, a four-number combination, produced "M-A-R-Y." That made no sense. How could a lady's name lead to a vault full of gold and silver?

Lucas tried another combination, four numbers in a row again, but only got "L-L-S-I," a string of letters that meant nothing to him.

He tried the final series of four numbers. The string was "428-380-411-386," followed by a "58," a number he didn't have, and then "377."

The first four numbers produced "M-O-C-C." Lucas spoke the sound out loud. Only one word came to mind.

Moccasin.

Like *Moccasin Hollow.* Was the treasure buried somewhere in Creech's snake-filled hollow?

He skipped to the number 377. "Silence." An *S.* Leaving a blank for the fifty-eighth word, it gave him "MOCC_S."

It fit. *Moccasin* worked.

In the cipher's next-to-last line, he found a 404, a 409, and a 374 together. The three corresponding words from

Annie's poem were "on," "ancient," and "keep." An *O*, an *A*, and a *K*.

Oak.

Suddenly Lucas Whitlatch had a pretty good idea where the treasure of Thomas Jefferson Beale lay buried.

CHAPTER 29

Just then George bounded up onto the porch and through the screen door, a towel wrapped around his shoulders, his wet hair matted to his freckled forehead.

"Hey, I thought you were zip-lining with me. What are you doing? Why are you smiling at me like that?" Then his mouth dropped open. "Hey! That's my toilet paper!"

"We have to go back," said Lucas.

"Sorry, dude, you missed your chance," said George. "They just shut it down for the day."

"Not the zip line, George. Back to Creech's farm."

George was dumbstruck. "Are you insane?"

Lucas held up the strip of toilet paper he'd used to jot down the few decoded words from Cipher One. "It's the treasure, George."

"Uh, Lucas, that's toilet paper," replied the younger boy, now certain that his friend had gone crazy. "I mean, it's awful important to me and all, but I wouldn't exactly call it *treasure*."

"No, you idiot," exclaimed Lucas, "not the toilet paper. The words!"

He quickly but calmly explained how Creech had retrieved the box in the middle of the night and how he himself had ended up with a page from Annie Morris's book. Then Lucas showed George the copy of the ciphers from the store and the notes he'd made while decoding Cipher One with the poem.

"That treasure is somewhere on that farm, and it's gotta be near the old oak tree, maybe right under it," Lucas concluded. "I mean, why else would it say *moccasin* and *oak* right at the end of the code? If you're following the directions, that's where you're supposed to end up."

George had listened intently. He fingered the page from the old book and held it up toward Lucas.

"But if this book already has numbers in it, Mr. Creech must know it was used for a code. Wouldn't he have the treasure by now?"

"I already thought about that," replied Lucas. "If he does, where is it? I mean, does he look like a millionaire to you?"

"I don't know, Lucas," said George, looking at the page again. "Maybe someone else used this book and found it a long time ago."

"There ain't nobody but Creech and his kin who could've even *seen* that book. It's like Maggie said; it's one of a kind."

George pondered that for a few seconds "Okay, then one of his old relatives found it, and it's long gone."

"I thought about that too, and it don't make any sense. I mean, if he found the treasure, why wouldn't Mr. Creech tell everybody? Why's he keep saying the story's a fake? I mean, he could just tell everybody the treasure's been found, show 'em some kind of evidence, and then everybody'd leave him alone like he wants. I'm tellin' you, George, that treasure is still sittin' in the ground somewhere near that oak tree. Either that or Mr. Creech knows a lot more about it than he's tellin' us. Either way, I aim to find out."

But even as he said it, a part of him still wondered if he'd become so desperate he'd believe anything about the treasure. But then he thought about returning to Indian Hole in less than a day, to a mountain that was going to disappear forever—the mountain his father had told him to look after. If the treasure was still buried somewhere on the old man's property, just a small part of it could save his mountain. And if it wasn't, if Creech already had it, then the old man was the only person he knew who might be able to help him. Either way, he had to see Creech again.

Lucas looked at his friend and added, "I got to, George."

"Okay," George replied, "so let's say there's a tiny little chance you're right. And I mean tiny. Even if I thought it was a good idea, how are you supposed to get back there? You're going home tomorrow morning."

Lucas knew George was right. His grandma wasn't going to hear any more talk about treasure either. Once he got picked up from camp, he'd never get another chance at it. He stared down at his notes once more, and the letters stared back: *MOCC_S__, OAK*. Behind the cabin, he heard the sound of Aaron buzzing by on the four-wheeler.

"Then we go back by ourselves," he said.

"Are you crazy? It took us three days last time!" said George. "And why do you keep saying *we*?"

"It took us three days to *walk*," Lucas countered. "But we're not going to walk."

All of a sudden it hit George. "You're going to steal the truck? You can't even drive!"

"You're right," said Lucas. "I can't drive a truck. But I can drive a four-wheeler. Aaron's four-wheeler."

The buzz of the four-wheeler had died to an idle as Aaron pulled it to a stop up the road. "And we're not stealing. We're *borrowing*."

"Whoa," said George. "That thing's only got room for one. And why would I go off and get lost with you again anyway?"

"It's got that little trailer on the back, George. You can ride in it."

"No way!"

"C'mon, George. I need you to help me find my way back. Plus, I don't want to head up into Creech's place by myself." He saw the fear enter the younger boy's eyes at the thought of facing the old man again. "Look, all we're going to do is talk to him one more time. We'll be back here before dark."

George went quiet and paced across the cabin floor, shaking his head. "But what about dinner?" he finally blurted.

"I think that can be part of the plan," replied Lucas, and then he worked out the rest of it.

CHAPTER 30

When the dinner bell rang at six o'clock sharp, Lucas perched on his bunk to wait, while George took up his position on the front porch. Lucas heard the doors of the other cabins slamming and the chattering of campers crossing the lawn and heading for the dining hall. Part of him wished he could join them. He hadn't eaten anything since Creech's breakfast at the crack of dawn, so he tried not to think of the food he'd be missing. He was happy George had made it to lunch at least. He doubted the younger boy would have skipped another meal to head back to Moccasin Hollow, and dinnertime was their only chance to escape.

A minute after the bell rang, George slipped back into the cabin.

"Okay, they're coming," he said, before disappearing back out onto the porch.

Lucas scooted under his bunk, cramming himself tightly

against the wall while George pulled the covers down to hide him better. A few seconds later, he heard Maggie's voice from out in the lawn.

"Dinnertime, George. You and Lucas, c'mon."

"Lucas is still in the shower, but he'll be out any second. We'll be up there as soon as he's dressed."

Lucas was hoping the delay would give them at least a half-hour head start back to Creech's.

"Tell you what, George." It was Aaron's voice. "Why don't you go on up, and I'll wait on Lucas. I know you're starving."

George paused long enough to make Lucas think the offer of a hot meal would be enough to make the younger boy abandon their plan. Finally, George spoke up, "I'll hurry him up. I *never* miss dinner. Well, unless I'm stuck in a cave, I guess."

There was silence for a moment, and Lucas wondered if the counselors were afraid to leave them alone after their last escape.

Finally, Maggie said, "Okay, George, we'll make sure they save something for you. Just don't be too late. The last dinner is kind of a big deal."

"Oh, don't worry!" George said cheerfully. It was another minute before he came through the door. "Okay, they're gone. Thanks for making me the big liar again."

Lucas immediately threw the blanket off and popped up from the bunk. "They goin' up the hill?"

"Yeah, but something's got them all charged up," said George. "They were talking up a storm the whole way."

"Probably still mad at us for runnin' off," said Lucas.

"Naw, I don't think it's that. More like really happy."

"Well, good for them if they are, but we gotta go."

"Are we really doing this?" asked George, giving Lucas one last chance to come to his senses.

"We have to," said Lucas, lacing up his boots. "Let's go."

They went out the back and jogged up the entrance road to the office. Across from the parking area was a three-sided shed where Aaron stored the four-wheeler. The trailer was already attached, but George checked to make sure it was secure while Lucas unloaded a half-dozen cans of paint to make room for a rider. He hopped into the seat and was relieved to see the key in the ignition. The camp's four-wheeler was a little different than the ones he'd ridden before, but looking over the various switches on the handlebars, he convinced himself he could figure out how to drive it.

"Jump on," he said to George.

George clambered into the little trailer and sat facing forward, his hands immediately clutching the rails in a white-knuckled death grip, even though the engine wasn't running yet.

Lucas turned the key to the start position and pushed a button labeled "Start." The engine began to turn over but didn't catch. He tried the button again, but the engine only sputtered.

"Gas?" guessed George.

Lucas unscrewed the gas cap on the tank between his knees. He rocked the four-wheeler so that he could see the fuel sloshing around. The tank was at least half-full.

"Nope. It's something else," he said. He knew they were losing valuable time. Aaron wouldn't wait until dinner was over to come looking for them.

He flicked another button, but it only turned the lights on and off.

George got out of the trailer. "How 'bout this one?" he said confidently. He jammed his thumb down on another button in the center of the handlebars.

The four-wheeler's horn blasted across the valley.

"Jeez, George!" whispered Lucas frantically. "It's *only* got a picture of a horn on it!"

They jumped behind one wall of the shed and peered up the hill, waiting to see if the noise had alerted any of the counselors. After a full minute, they came out of hiding.

"It's gotta be something simple," said Lucas. He climbed back into the driver's seat and noticed another switch above the start button. He flicked the switch up and then tried the button again.

The engine turned over once and began idling steadily.

"It's the kill switch, for shutting off the engine," he explained to George. "We gotta flip it back on to start it up. You ready?"

George climbed back onto the trailer and grabbed the rails.

The engine seemed loud in the quiet valley, but Lucas also knew how noisy the dining hall was at dinnertime. Just to be sure though, he puttered down the entrance road at a crawl, making sure not to rev the engine until they were well out of earshot. No one would hear them leave.

At the end of the camp's long entrance road, Lucas turned onto the highway that headed over the crest of the Blue Ridge and gave the four-wheeler some gas. The little machine kept moving, but its engine revved so high that he thought it might explode. With his left foot, Lucas lifted up the shifter to find a higher gear. The front wheels jumped off the ground, and the four-wheeler jerked forward so hard that George lost his grip and somersaulted backward off the little trailer. He landed on his feet on the pavement but tumbled backward onto his rear end.

"Jeez, I thought you said you could drive one of these things!" he yelled. He scrambled to his feet and ran to the shoulder where Lucas had pulled off. He examined the back of one arm and sucked a breath in through his teeth. "Jeez, that hurt!" He had a raw and bloody scrape the size of a half-dollar on his elbow.

"Sorry, George, this one is a little different."

Just then a big RV lumbered up the road past them. Lucas hadn't counted on dealing with other vehicles. He had to get to Creech's quick, but the four-wheeler wouldn't keep up with real traffic, especially hauling George and the trailer. He'd have to pull to the shoulder any time a car came up behind them.

George dabbed at his bloody elbow with his T-shirt and brushed some gravel off his backside.

"You want to go back?" asked Lucas. "You could walk it from here."

George's eyes were watering a little, and Lucas could see him think about it for a second. But the younger boy clenched his jaw and shook his head.

"Good," said Lucas. "Sit facing backward this time. That way you can tell me if there's a car coming."

"Sure," George grumbled, "and that way I can *face*-plant instead of *butt*-plant."

Once George was aboard, Lucas pulled the four-wheeler back onto the road and immediately found second gear. Every time he switched gears, the machine lurched violently, and George let out a little shriek, but Lucas quickly got the hang of driving it.

He only had to pull off twice for cars before they made it to the crest and started down the other side. At the top, Lucas yelled to George to hang on and finally put the four-wheeler into high gear. Before long, they were going almost as fast as a car could on the twisting road, but Lucas was still anxious to get off the highway and onto the back roads where the little machine belonged. He guessed the first turn to Creech's was only a few miles from the ridge. Lucas hollered at George over his shoulder.

"Do you remember where we turn?" he asked.

"Pull over!" George yelled back.

"Not yet, George," Lucas hollered back. "I think it's still up a ways."

"No! Get off the road! Now!"

A roaring from behind him made Lucas glance over his shoulder.

An enormous logging truck was barreling down the mountain and gaining on them fast.

Lucas started to wheel the four-wheeler to the side of the road, but the shoulder had disappeared. On his side, a face of rock crowded the yellow line, and across the other lane the hillside fell off steeply behind a guardrail. There was nowhere to go but forward. Lucas tried to slow to take a curve, but a blast from the massive truck's air horn echoed off the rocks next to him. He gave the four-wheeler more gas.

"Faster!" screamed George.

"I can't," Lucas shot back. "I'll lose it!"

The truck bore down on them. When the horn wailed again, the noise was so close that Lucas almost lost his grip on the handlebars.

"He's nuts!" yelled George.

The truck's brakes hissed just behind them. Lucas scanned the shoulders frantically, looking for even the smallest space to bail off the road.

Suddenly, a yellow sign appeared in the trees and shot by. *Runaway Truck Ramp 1,000 Feet.*

Lucas had seen the ramps back home—a giant stair step of sand built to stop a truck with overheated brakes. He saw the opening on the shoulder at the end of a long straight-away and squeezed the throttle, pulling ahead of the eighteen-wheeler for just a second.

But the trucker was fed up. Despite the double yellow line down the center of the road, he eased the big rig out into the center of the road.

"Slow down, Lucas!" hollered George. "He's going around!"

The truck started past them, so close that Lucas smelled the freshly logged timber piled on its trailer. He let off the gas a little, and the truck began to slip by faster.

But before it could pass them, a motorcycle roared around the curve in the oncoming lane. The massive truck's brakes hissed and the rig jerked back into Lucas's lane, forcing him off the road just as they reached the little opening for the ramp.

"Hold on, George!" Lucas screamed over the sound of screeching brakes and a final warning blast of the truck's horn. But George was screaming too loud to hear him, as the truck's big tires nearly grazed the edge of his tiny trailer.

Lucas jerked the wheel to the right, and the four-wheeler plunged off the road and onto the ramp, out of control.

CHAPTER 31

At first they seemed to glide across the top of the gravelly sand. But when Lucas hit the brakes, the front wheels of the four-wheeler sunk in, and they jolted to a brutal stop. Lucas flew over the handlebars. George's trailer jackknifed upward, shooting him high into the air, still screaming. Ten feet beyond the four-wheeler, they tumbled to a stop in the ramp's deep bed sand.

For a few seconds, they lay there, staring up at the clouds and listening to the growling gears of the truck winding down the mountain. Lucas started to ask if George was all right when a radio on their little machine crackled to life.

"Lucas…George…out there?" It was Maggie's voice, masked by static and breaking up.

Lucas sat up. He hadn't noticed the radio before, but now he saw it strapped below the dashboard, its red light glowing when Maggie spoke.

"I don't know…you boys are up to…where you are."

The radio clicked off for a second, then Aaron's voice came through the static, angrier.

"…wheeler better be…one piece!"

George scrambled to his feet, but Lucas stopped him.

"Just ignore it, George. We answer, and we're going to have to tell 'em where we are. They'll pick us up before we get to Moccasin Hollow."

"If we even *get* to Moccasin Hollow," George groaned. He brushed some sand out of his hair and checked himself for more scrapes. "We almost got killed!"

"A few more minutes, and we'll be on back roads, George. No more trucks."

Before he hopped back into the driver seat, Lucas reached down and clicked off the radio. It took them a few minutes to dislodge the four-wheeler from the deep sand, but aside from some fresh scratches on the front fenders, it was still in good shape.

They took a right turn onto the dirt road at the cross-roads where Lucas had seen the old woman selling honey that morning. There was no sign of her now, just her clapboard stand and the logs with the empty, sagging board between them. Lucas stopped the four-wheeler in the little gravel lot and let the engine idle. He read the historical marker across the road.

St. Mary's Chapel, established on this site in 1798. Destroyed by fire 1864.

Lucas recalled the other letters he'd been able to decipher and pointed to the sign.

"I think Beale used the church in his directions," he told George.

"How do you know?"

"M-A-R-Y was in the code too. Like the girl's name—Mary. I bet it said *St. Mary's*."

"Kind of a stretch if you ask me," said George skeptically.

Lucas pointed out the narrow concrete bridge that had taken them onto the road to Creech's farm, and ten minutes after crossing the creek, they rounded a curve and spied the wide spot in the road where the ambulance and Maggie's truck had been parked. Creech's mailbox sat next to a tree tacked with a NO TRESPASSING sign. Where the sign had read, VIOLATORS WILL BE PROSECUTED, Creech had scratched out PROSECUTED and painted SHOT! in bold red letters.

Through a jungle of blackberries and wild roses at the edge of the road, Lucas could just make out the trail to Creech's house. If he hadn't used it that morning, he would never have seen it.

He glanced at the sun. It was only a couple hours from the top of the ridge across the valley from Moccasin Hollow. Two hours till dark.

"We'll drive up the trail," he told George. "It'll save time."

"Aren't we trespassing? Again?"

"You remember what Maggie said. It's mostly an act."

"Yeah, *mostly*," said George doubtfully. "Maybe he's *mostly* a bad shot too." Still, he stayed on the trailer, and Lucas started up the rough path. They took it slow up Creech's narrow trail, and after a few minutes, they broke out of the woods, bringing the house into view across the broad meadow. Lucas scanned the farm for any sign of Creech. He half expected to see the old man burst out onto his front porch, gun in hand, but he was nowhere in sight.

Lucas looked at the giant tree rising from behind the house. No other tree in sight was even half as old. It had to be the oak from the code.

He tried to imagine the scene as Beale had seen it. No farm, no house, only the lonely oak watching over the mouth of a wild hollow at the foot of the Blue Ridge. A solitary guard watching over Beale's treasure.

They crossed the final hundred yards to the house and parked the ATV by the front steps. Creech was nowhere to be seen, so they stepped up onto the porch. The front door was open, letting them see through the screen into the parlor. They listened for a few seconds but heard no sound from inside the house. Lucas rapped on the screen door and called out the old man's name. Then he did it again louder, but still there was no response.

"I guess we try around back," he said.

There was no sign of him there either. Behind the house, the only movement came from the leaves of the orchard trees whispering in the breeze pouring down from the mountains above the hollow. The two boys stopped beneath the canopy of the huge oak and scanned the rest of the little farm. For all they knew, the old man was way up in the hollow, miles away.

"Maybe he went back up there to get his shotgun," George ventured, pointing up into the mountains.

"If he did, he's gotta be back before dark," Lucas replied. Still, he knew if Creech didn't return soon, they'd never have time to get back to camp before nightfall—or before Maggie or Aaron tracked them down first.

And just because Lucas was certain this was the oak from the cipher, the treasure could be anywhere near the big tree. Only the rest of Annie Morris's book would tell him exactly where, but that was locked up tight in Creech's desk. And if it wasn't still in the ground, if Creech somehow had it, there was still a chance the old man would help him. Either way, he needed Creech to show up soon.

Just then, a crow cawed from the big rock looming behind the outhouse.

"Or maybe he's in there," George said, pointing at the little shed under the rock.

"He's got a real bathroom, remember?" said Lucas. "Why would he be in there?"

It was the first time Lucas had paid much attention to the outhouse. From where they stood, he could see a tiny window in the shape of a moon carved in its door. Like the main house, the little shack was well cared for, with fresh paint and a solid-looking roof.

Why care for an old outhouse if you don't even need it anymore?

It was built right up against the big rock too, where it would have been next to impossible to dig the hole. *And uphill from the house?*

"That outhouse don't even make sense, George."

"If you say so, Lucas," replied George. "I mean, no offense, but you've probably got a little more outhouse experience than me."

"Yeah, I do," replied Lucas, still staring at the little outbuilding, "and I ain't ever seen one uphill of a house and built right next to a big ol' rock."

"So what are you saying?"

Lucas grinned at George. "I'm saying maybe that ain't no outhouse. But maybe it's a hole."

Before George could reply, Lucas was sprinting uphill toward the little shack.

CHAPTER 32

Lucas stopped outside the outhouse and waited for George to catch up. Aside from the buzz of a yellow jacket flying out through the little moon cut out of the door, there was no sound from inside.

George, still panting, extended his hand toward the door. "You first."

Lucas peeked through the moon, but the inside was as black as a cave. The cool air wafting from the little window smelled only of earth and wood, definitely not the stench of a real outhouse. He grabbed the door's rough wood handle and pulled.

The outhouse faced east, away from the setting sun, so the interior of the little shack was still shadowy and dim. Lucas half expected to see a secret staircase or a ladder leading underground, but instead they found an old, well-worn bench with a hole in the center, just like a real outhouse. Hanging above the bench, a brittle shell of skin shed by a long, fat snake was draped over a ceiling beam like a warning, the kind of spooky thing Creech would have left there to scare someone out of the place. Lucas looked back at the hole in the bench.

"We need a flashlight," he said. "At least we could see what's down there."

Lucas stepped into the tiny structure and moved to one side, so some daylight could penetrate the pit beneath the seat. He tried to look into the hole, but the light only fell a few inches inside. Beyond that, the hole was so black it could have been bottomless.

"George," Lucas said, never taking his eyes off the hole, "does that watch light up?"

"Whoa, wait a minute." George protested.

"I need a light."

George unbuckled the bulky wristwatch and handed it to Lucas. "My mom gave me that watch, Lucas. Drop it in that hole, and I swear you're going in after it," he said. "Even if you have to scuba dive in dookie."

"Just show me which button."

George took the watch and pressed a button on the side. The watch's face glowed a dim blue.

"That ain't much light, but it's somethin'," said Lucas, taking the watch back from him.

He poked the watch down into the hole but immediately

felt his hand encased in spiderwebs. When he pulled it out, a fat black widow was dangling from the watch strap.

"Dang!" he shouted and flung the spider out into the sunlight, just past George's face.

"Jesus!" said George. "Is it on me?!"

"No, it went flying." Lucas wrenched a splinter of lumber from one of the floor planks and poked it into the hole, stirring it around to knock down any more webs. He tossed the stick into the hole and heard it hit bottom a second later. Holding the watch down in the hole again, he hit the button for the light. The beam only illuminated a few feet of swirling dust. Below that was nothing but black.

"Not enough," he said.

He backed out just far enough to see the sun. It wasn't far from the top of the trees along a distant ridge. They'd be out of sunlight in an hour. Lucas angled the watch to catch the sun's rays and carefully moved it until its reflection found the bench. After a few tries, he directed the little beam of light into the hole and held it steady.

"Look down in there and see if you see anything," he told George.

The younger boy went into the outhouse and stood to the side of the light beam. He leaned over and peered in the hole.

"There's just dirt," he said. "Or at least I hope that's dirt."

He moved his head a little closer to the hole. "Wait a minute. Move it a little lower. There. Hold it steady."

George turned to look at his friend.

"Lucas, there's something bright down there."

Lucas's breath caught in his throat. His hands shook as he tried to keep the watch focused down the hole.

"George, you hold it and let me look."

They switched positions, and in a few seconds, George had the reflection shining down the hole again. Lucas watched as the narrow circle of light fell on something solid and white.

"That's just quartz rock. Definitely not gold."

"Silver maybe?" asked George.

"Just rock," replied Lucas. "But looks like a bunch of them stacked up like a wall."

Then Lucas remembered the words from Beale's description: *The vault is roughly lined with stones...*

"Move it around a little, George."

The beam of light dropped down below the wall of rocks and fell on something rusty.

"Right there, George!"

It was some kind of metal container, maybe the size of a basketball, topped with a lid. And there were others around it.

...securely packed in iron pots with iron covers...

"There's pots down there! Just like in the story!" shouted Lucas, kicking the bench in his excitement.

One of the planks on the front of the bench clattered to the wood floor, and a sunbeam over George's shoulder cast its light through the swirling dust all the way to the bottom of the hole.

Dozens of iron pots covered in orange rust were stacked in neat rows at the bottom of the pit.

The treasure vault was exactly as Beale had described it.

Lucas braced himself and pried a plank off the top of the bench. It was hardly even nailed in place, as if Creech were making it easy for someone to get to the treasure.

Together, they knocked loose the other boards that formed the bench and propped them against the wall. Every board they removed let more of the day's dying light into the hole, revealing a vault walled in on three sides with carefully stacked chunks of white quartz.

The pit was dug several feet under the sloping rock that jutted from the hillside outside, forming a rough, natural ceiling for the back half of the vault. Half of the floor, six feet down, was covered in the round, metal pots.

Lucas wanted to jump straight in, but he was afraid he'd land on the pots. "Here," he said to George, "lower me down."

Lucas flopped onto his belly and dangled his legs over the edge of the dark hole. He braced one hand against one wall of the outhouse while George held on to his other hand and lowered him in.

"I can't catch my breath," said George.

Lucas felt it too—gold fever. When he dropped onto the dirt floor of the vault, his head was spinning, and he had to stop for a few seconds to calm down.

"Which one should I open?" he asked George, hovering over the rusty kettles.

"Hey, you found it. *You* pick."

Lucas grabbed the lid of one of the pots closest to him and began to pull.

It was rusted shut.

"Hold on," called George, disappearing from view. When he returned, he tossed a fist-sized rock into the vault next to Lucas. "Try hitting it with that."

Lucas struck the edge of the lid a few times and finally saw it give a little. He grasped the lid and pulled again. This time it gave way, and he turned the heavy pot to the light.

Empty.

He banged away at another lid and knocked it off. Another empty one.

The next lid he tried came off easily.

Nothing.

He began frantically shoving aside the empty pots to get at the ones in the back. But each one he tried was filled with nothing but a handful of powdery orange rust. He had opened more than half the pots in the vault before he heard

George yelling his name.

"Lucas! Lucas, stop! There's nothing there."

But Lucas was nearly delirious. He kept scattering lids and empty pots, banging open the ones that might still be hiding gold or silver.

There has to be something!

"Lucas. Listen! You need to stop…Lucas!"

The tremble in George's voice brought him out of his frenzy. When he turned away from the jumble of pots and lids and looked up into the light, he saw that George's eyes were rimmed with tears. He realized he was crying himself.

There's nothing left.

Nothing.

"Come on, Lucas," George whimpered, "just get out of the hole."

George reached out a hand to help Lucas up the side. Outside, squinting in the fading sunlight, Lucas began angrily knocking the dirt off his clothes, hollering as he did.

"He's a liar! That mean old snake is nothin' but a liar!" He screamed toward the mountains and then at the house, hoping Creech could hear him. "GIDDY CREECH AIN'T NOTHIN' BUT A LYIN', STINKIN' SNAKE!"

With the final word, he spun around and gave the outhouse wall a kick that snapped a plank loose. It felt good, breaking something that belonged to the old man, felt like he was kicking Creech himself. So Lucas reared back to give the shack another kick, this one even harder, figuring he'd turn the old man's outhouse into a pile of splinters.

But a voice, rough and familiar, stopped him before he could.

"Son, I hope you ain't gonna tear down my old johnny house. It's sorta sentimental."

Gideon Creech stood on top of the rocks above the outhouse, his shotgun cradled across his chest.

CHAPTER 33

Spry as a mountain goat, Creech hopped down off the rocks and leaned the shotgun against the outhouse. With a glance inside the little shack, he surveyed the damage they'd done. But instead of being furious, he smiled a real smile at them for the very first time.

"I figured that little book of mine was missin' a page. Looks like you did a little code crackin' from it too." He glanced at the four-wheeler parked under the tree. "And you come all the way back here on that little thing too?" Creech shook his head. "Awful headstrong, ain't you, son?"

"So what happened to the treasure?" Lucas asked, still angry that his efforts had amounted to nothing and that Creech had known all along.

"Well," replied Creech, "that's a long story. But a lot of it went back to them explorers' families a long time ago, at least the ones that could be found. Then a lot of what was left bought some of these mountains. About twenty thousand acres' worth, in fact."

"Twenty thousand acres!" George exclaimed. "So the money is just sitting there? Doing nothing?"

"Hold on, boy," the old man shot back. "Keepin' a big chunk of these mountains from gettin' logged or mined or turned into some kind of fancy resort for city folks ain't exactly doin' nothin'. The way I see it, I'm gettin' a pretty good return on my investment leavin' it just like it is. That and lettin' it help a few kids now and then."

"What do you mean?" asked Lucas, but then it dawned on him. *Twenty thousand acres. Same as the camp.* "The camp? Camp Kawani belongs to *you?*"

Creech folded his arms over his chest and a crooked grin escaped his face. "Yep."

Lucas's jaw dropped open and he stared at George. So Creech really was rich. But owning a camp to help a bunch of kids was about the last thing he'd expected. Creech went on.

"See, when I was a boy, just about your age, my own mother passed away. Died sudden too, like your parents did. I didn't know it then, but after I grew up, I saw how this place is what kept me survivin' in that bad time. Sure I still had my father, but he had more than me to worry about, so he couldn't be around much. And as lonesome as it is here, well, those rocky knobs up there, this creek, even that big ol' tree over there, I guess they're what brought me back to life after a pretty bad time. They showed me this life's just too danged full a' wonders to give up on just because you lose a part of yours. It just takes some time and quiet to see that for yourself. 'Course keepin' these mountains from gettin' ruined ain't a bad idea either."

Lucas understood now what Creech meant—maybe trying to save the mountain above Indian Hole meant that he'd known it all along. And maybe he still had one last chance.

"Mr. Creech," he said, "I need your help with somethin' else, and I got nobody else to ask."

Lucas told him about his mountain, describing it with the same reverence Creech had for Moccasin Hollow and the wilderness around it, how it had been a part of his family for two hundred years and a part of him for as long as he could remember. "But it's about to be sold and torn apart, and it's all I got left." Confessing his own desperate future and giving up what little pride he had left to the old man made it hard to keep his voice from quivering and the tears from spilling out again.

"I hear you, son," Creech finally said, "but I don't think you need my help."

"Why?" asked Lucas, thinking, *I don't need another useless speech.*

"Why don't you and George go on over there and sit in the shade? I need to get somethin' from the house."

Creech picked up his shotgun and headed for the house. When he returned, he was carrying Annie Morris's book of poems. A folded sheet of paper and a stubby pencil were sticking out of the pages.

"Need you to do a little more decodin'," he said, handing Lucas the book. "Just the first twenty-five numbers."

Lucas opened the book and pulled out the sheet of paper. *Cipher Number Three: Names and Residences.* The first twenty-five numbers were underlined.

"Why Mr. Creech?" Lucas asked.

"Because that cipher there is the most important one," Creech said.

"Jeez, Lucas, just do it," said George. "We still gotta get back to camp, you know."

Creech only nodded.

Lucas sat down with his back against the big oak. He handed the code and the pencil to George who was already sitting in the grass. He still didn't see how this wasn't just a waste of time. "Okay," he said to George, "you give me the numbers and I'll find the letters."

"The first one's eighteen," said George.

Inside the fragile book, the little numbers were scrawled above every tenth word, just like on the loose page that had led him back to Moccasin Hollow. They were so faint that he could hardly make them out in the fading evening light, but

Lucas found the eighteenth word on the first page. The word was *garden.* "*G,*" he said. "Write that down."

"Okay, the next one is 224."

Lucas found the word in the second poem. *Under.* "It's a *U,*" he said, thinking *G-U. That spells exactly nothing.*

Three letters later, they had the letters G-U-I-D-E.

"Guide," said George. "At least it spells something."

"Yeah, but what's it got to do with me?" said Lucas, looking at Creech.

The old man only nodded at the book, silently urging him to keep going.

George gave him the next one, "422."

Lucas gently turned the fragile pages and saw that the word he needed was on the page he'd stolen. He fished into his pocket and unfolded the brittle paper, looking guiltily at Creech. "It's right here," he said to George. "Ring," he said. "It's an *R.*"

George fed him the next six numbers and wrote the letters down in silence. Finally, George looked up at Creech, then back at the paper. "The next one's 387," he said, "but I bet it's a *T.*"

Lucas scanned the loose page for the word and found it.

The word was *tall.* A *T.*

"How'd you figure that?" he asked George.

"Lucas, it's spelling out your name." He shoved the paper

in front of Lucas's face for him to read. George had written "G-U-I-D-E-R-W-H-I-T-L-A-T." "The next two are 34 and 155, but you know they're going to be a *C* and an *H*."

Lucas looked them up, turning the pages a bit more urgently. George was right.

The code spelled out "G-U-I-D-E-R-W-H-I-T-L-A-T-C-H."

Guide R. Whitlatch.

"Who's R. Whitlatch?" Lucas said.

"Lucas," George said, "maybe you're related to the treasure somehow."

"Yeah, but that name don't mean nothin'," Lucas replied. He looked toward Creech, whose face showed no emotion.

"There's ten more numbers underlined," said George. "You wanna decode them?"

"Yeah, give 'em to me."

The first was a forty-three, so it was in one of the first lines on the first page of the book. The forty-third word was *inside*. An *I*. George kept writing.

Lucas found the next number in a poem called "Stars." It went with the word *nightfall*. "It's an *N*," he said to George.

The next letter was a *D*.

Four letters later, Lucas began to understand why the old man had been so anxious to retrieve the old box from his desk in the middle of the night.

Lucas lifted his gaze from the pages of Annie Morris's little book and stared at the old man. Creech was grinning from ear to ear, his own eyes watering a bit. He was nodding slowly, telling Lucas to believe what he was seeing.

"Go on," the old man said softly. "Spell out the rest."

Lucas knew for certain what the rest of the numbers would tell him, but he deciphered them anyway, shaking his head in disbelief with every new letter. By the time he found the last one, his hands were shaking too.

George pointed to the letters they'd scrawled on the paper. "Mr. Creech," he asked, "does this mean what I think it does?"

Creech was staring at Lucas instead. A tear welled from his eye and trailed down the old man's cheek into his dirty white whiskers.

George handed the paper to Lucas.

It read: *GUIDE R WHITLATCH INDIAN HOLE.*

CHAPTER 34

Creech told them how Randall Whitlatch, Lucas's own great-great-great grandfather, had been Beale's guide and why the Whitlatches had been so hard to find. For one, Indian Hole didn't exist on any map, old or new. It was simply what the Whitlatches and maybe a few others had called their remote home since before even Randall's time. And since the rest of Beale's men were Virginians from east of the Blue Ridge, Beale hadn't bothered to write down a state for any of them, so no one had even looked way out in West Virginia. Besides, even if Beale had added a state for Randall, he'd have written "Virginia" since West Virginia was just another part of Virginia back then anyway.

"It wasn't till you all stumbled down into Moccasin Hollow," Creech said, "and told me you were from a place called Indian Hole that I remembered them words from the codes. Remembered the guide's name sounded like whiplash too. Got Beale's old box out last night and made sure of it. I told Maggie what I found out this morning, and your grandma certified it, Lucas. Maggie stopped by to tell me on her way back from the hospital."

Then Creech explained how Annie Morris had fallen in love with Thomas Jefferson Beale that first winter he'd stayed at the old inn and how she'd died giving birth to their baby, Creech's great-great grandma. That was why the key was never brought to the innkeeper—his own daughter was supposed to tell him to use her little book of poetry, but that secret died with her.

"Wait, that means you're related to the explorer guy," George said.

"Yep," Creech said. "He was my third great grandpa. Their daughter, the one Annie died giving birth to, ended up with the codes, and she's the one that found them little numbers scrawled in her mother's poetry book. Found the treasure the same week. Then her and my great-great grandpa—he was a Creech—they used some of the innkeeper's share to build this house. Kept the treasure in the ground while they tried to find all them explorers' kin.

"But a lot of time had already passed and Beale hadn't exactly put a lot of details in the ciphers, so a lot of 'em she couldn't find. In the end, she got old sittin' on a big ol' pile of gold and silver. Same for her kids, right on down to my own father. Each generation searched and found a few of those families to give 'em their share, but by the time it got passed down to me, the rest of that treasure had been sittin' in a bank a long time, and it grew into a lot more money.

"'Course," added Creech, "I sort of liked the idea of preservin' ol' Beale's handiwork under that rock over there, seein' as it's the oldest piece of family history in this hollow. Didn't have the heart to just fill it in. So I built that fake johnny house to hide it under, figuring that'd be the last place anybody'd want to look for a buried treasure. And I left Beale's empty pots in the ground, figurin' if anyone ever *did* find it while I was gone, they'd just dig up a whole bunch of disappointment." He shrugged. "Sorry that ended up being you, Lucas."

"So what's it worth now?" George asked eagerly. "How much belongs to Lucas's family?"

Lucas was still trying to figure how he'd gotten so lucky that it hadn't even occurred to him to ask the same question.

"I'm gettin' around to that," Creech said, "but let me tell my story first. You see, I looked hard for near thirty years for just one of them explorers' families. Even used lawyers and computers and all, but I never even found a one. Always hated havin' all that money that belonged to someone else."

Lucas finally spoke up, sniffing the last of his tears away first. "So it's been in the bank all this time?"

"Well, some of it. And like I said, some of it's still right here in these mountains." He jabbed his thumb at the forested peaks rising up behind his house.

"And you said Maggie talked to my grandma for you?" asked Lucas.

"She does a lot of things for me," answered Creech. "Ought to. She's my granddaughter, after all."

The boys looked at each other, wide-eyed once more. "But Aaron's her brother," sputtered George, "That means he's…"

"My grandson? Yep. The two of them run that camp for me now. Do a pretty good job too—aside from losing a few campers lately and making me out to be some kinda scary snake man."

"So they both know about all this?" asked Lucas, holding up the paper.

"Sure do," said Creech. "That's why I reckon they'll be along any minute. They're bound to know exactly where you were headed when you ran off again."

"So why didn't they just tell me?" asked Lucas, thinking how they could have killed themselves getting back to Moccasin Hollow.

"Because you never gave me a *chance*," said a voice from behind them.

Maggie had come around the corner of the farmhouse. Aaron and another man were right behind her. The other man was on the chubby side, very red in the face and out of breath. Lucas knew with one look that he was George's pa.

George jumped up from the grass. "What the…Dad?" His father broke into a run as soon as he saw him and wrapped George in a sweaty bear hug. He began sobbing George's name so loudly that everyone but George seemed a little embarrassed. George just buried his face in his dad's shirt and started crying right along with him.

After the Funderburks calmed down, Maggie said, "Aaron and I were all set to tell you at dinner. We had a big announcement planned, but you took off. When Grandpa here told me what he knew this morning, I called Lucas's grandparents and asked them a lot of questions. This afternoon, his grandmother brought me everything she had about Randall Whitlatch. Born in 1791, disappeared out West with a hunting party in 1822. He's definitely the Whitlatch from Beale's codes."

"But what's it worth? Lucas's share, I mean," asked George again.

"Yeah, I have to say, I'm pretty curious about that myself," added his father anxiously.

"Well, first of all," said Maggie, "it's Lucas's grandfather's share—he's the oldest surviving descendant of Randall Whitlatch. But let's just say it's in the millions. Quite a few millions in fact."

"Dude," said George, "you're a millionaire!"

It dawned on Lucas then. The money meant a whole new life for everyone—but only because his pa had lost his. That thought was too much to bear. "Heck, I'd give all the money in the world to have him back," he muttered.

For a moment, the others were silent until Maggie finally spoke. "I know it's tough, Lucas, having your father pass away right before something fantastic like this happens to his family. But maybe it's like a gift. His gift. After all, you would never have been invited to our camp if he hadn't gone off to war. And Mr. Creech…Grandpa would never have found out about you."

"Yeah, Lucas," George chimed in, "you said up in that cave that your dad went off to fight to help you have a better life. I know it won't be the same without him, just like for me without my mom, but in a way that's what he ended up doing."

"And after your family's taken care of," added Maggie, "there's a lot of good that can be done with the kind of money you're getting. It can be set up in your father's name. Your grandmother's already got some ideas."

"Lucas," George exclaimed suddenly, "you know we gotta tell Alex about this! Is he still in the hospital?" he asked Maggie.

"Most likely," said Maggie. "We can take you there, I guess."

"What about camp though?" asked George. He turned to his father. "Lucas and I still have one more night."

"Fine with me," said Mr. Funderburk. "I'm not driving all the way back to Maryland tonight anyway. I can get a room in town and we'll head back tomorrow morning." He looked straight at his son, his eyes a little misty again, and added, "Together."

"Let's go then," said Maggie. "We need to get down Grandpa's trail here while there's still some light." She caught Creech's eye. "And your head's probably spinning from seeing so many other human beings today, right?"

"Enough for a whole year," replied the old man, but he winked at Lucas.

They all walked around to the front of the house in the last light of the day. Creech stood on the steps of his porch.

Aaron started up his four-wheeler, but not before scowling at the fresh scratches on its fender. "I'll get this loaded up," he said to Maggie, and motored off toward the road.

Maggie and the Funderburks started down the trail together, but Lucas hung back with Creech.

"Thank you, Mr. Creech," he said. "For everything."

"Well, you did the hard part yourself. If you hadn't come down that mountain tryin' to save your friends, I'd of never heard of Lucas Whitlatch of Indian Hole, West Virginia."

"I reckon, sir," said Lucas. "But even so, thanks."

"Take care of yourself, son," Creech said.

Lucas turned to join the others but realized he still had the loose page from Annie Morris's book of poetry. Walking back up to Creech, he handed him the wrinkled paper.

"Sorry about your book," he said.

Creech laughed. "Keep it. Call it a souvenir from your night in my little hotel here."

"No, sir," said Lucas. "It's yours. And it belongs with the others."

Creech took the page, and Lucas watched him read the verses.

"These mountains were special to her, weren't they?" he said to the old man.

Creech looked up from the poem. "I guess we both know about that, don't we?"

Lucas smiled and nodded. "Yes, sir." Then he turned to catch up.

Maggie had slowed to wait for him, and he met her halfway down the trail.

"Do you think he'll ever tell the truth about the treasure now, so no one bothers him anymore?" Lucas asked her.

"Maybe he will, now that he finally found someone who deserved a part of the money," she said. "Or maybe he'll keep the legend alive just so he can chase a few treasure hunters off his property every now and then. Sometimes I think he enjoys his reputation too much."

Just as they joined George and his father, a soft rumble from a thunderhead beyond the long ridge to the west rolled toward them across the valley of the Shenandoah. A moment later, a strong breeze brushed the tall grasses and stirred the yellow heads of the meadow flowers.

"I'm outta here," said George. "The last time I got caught in a storm with you, it wasn't exactly a picnic."

"I know," said Lucas. "Let's go."

But as the others headed for the gap in the trees that led to the road, he paused long enough for a final look at Moccasin Hollow and the mountains that had delivered him there. The farmhouse and the ancient oak tree were already deep in shadow, but the mountains above them were still painted with the last warm light of the day. He thought again about the poem from Annie's book, the one about heaven being right here. The one that could have also been about a mountain above Indian Hole, West Virginia. His mountain. A mountain that would forever be green and would always be home.

AUTHOR'S NOTE

I first heard the legend of the Beale Ciphers from my father while hiking in the mountains not far from where Thomas Jefferson Beale is alleged to have buried his treasure. Since then I've been fascinated with the idea of a fortune lying hidden in those same mountains I walked as a teenager.

Today, because even the most skilled cryptographers in the world have failed to decode Beale's other ciphers, most so-called experts believe the legend is an elaborate hoax. Still, many of those same experts admit that if the key is a rare document—perhaps something like Annie Morris's private book of poetry—the codes will never be broken, and the treasure, if it exists, will only be discovered by sheer luck.

As for myself, I am satisfied knowing that just enough lonely wilderness remains in the Blue Ridge Mountains of Virginia to hide a few secrets.

For the die-hard treasure seeker, I include here the actual

coded instructions for finding and distributing Beale's treasure. Only Cipher Two, "The Contents of the Vault," has been decoded so far. Cipher One, and some very good luck, may lead the reader to a fortune in gold, silver, and jewels.

CIPHER ONE
THE LOCATION OF THE VAULT

71, 194, 38, 1701, 89, 76, 11, 83, 1629, 48, 94, 63, 132,
16, 111, 95, 84, 341, 975, 14, 40, 64, 27, 81, 139, 213, 63,
90, 1120, 8, 15, 3, 126, 2018, 40, 74, 758, 485, 604, 230,
436, 664, 582, 150, 251, 284, 308, 231, 124, 211, 486, 225,
401, 370, 11, 101, 305, 139, 189, 17, 33, 88, 208, 193, 145,
1, 94, 73, 416, 918, 263, 28, 500, 538, 356, 117, 136, 219,
27, 176, 130, 10, 460, 25, 485, 18, 436, 65, 84, 200, 283,
118, 320, 138, 36, 416, 280, 15, 71, 224, 961, 44, 16, 401,
39, 88, 61, 304, 12, 21, 24, 283, 134, 92, 63, 246, 486,
682, 7, 219, 184, 360, 780, 18, 64, 463, 474, 131, 160, 79,
73, 440, 95, 18, 64, 581, 34, 69, 128, 367, 460, 17, 81, 12,
103, 820, 62, 116, 97, 103, 862, 70, 60, 1317, 471, 540,
208, 121, 890, 346, 36, 150, 59, 568, 614, 13, 120, 63, 219,
812, 2160, 1780, 99, 35, 18, 21, 136, 872, 15, 28, 170, 88,
4, 30, 44, 112, 18, 147, 436, 195, 320, 37, 122, 113, 6, 140,
8, 120, 305, 42, 58, 461, 44, 106, 301, 13, 408, 680, 93, 86,

116, 530, 82, 568, 9, 102, 38, 416, 89, 71, 216, 728, 965, 818, 2, 38, 121, 195, 14, 326, 148, 234, 18, 55, 131, 234, 361, 824, 5, 81, 623, 48, 961, 19, 26, 33, 10, 1101, 365, 92, 88, 181, 275, 346, 201, 206, 86, 36, 219, 324, 829, 840, 64, 326, 19, 48, 122, 85, 216, 284, 919, 861, 326, 985, 233, 64, 68, 232, 431, 960, 50, 29, 81, 216, 321, 603, 14, 612, 81, 360, 36, 51, 62, 194, 78, 60, 200, 314, 676, 112, 4, 28, 18, 61, 136, 247, 819, 921, 1060, 464, 895, 10, 6, 66, 119, 38, 41, 49, 602, 423, 962, 302, 294, 875, 78, 14, 23, 111, 109, 62, 31, 501, 823, 216, 280, 34, 24, 150, 1000, 162, 286, 19, 21, 17, 340, 19, 242, 31, 86, 234, 140, 607, 115, 33, 191, 67, 104, 86, 52, 88, 16, 80, 121, 67, 95, 122, 216, 548, 96, 11, 201, 77, 364, 218, 65, 667, 890, 236, 154, 211, 10, 98, 34, 119, 56, 216, 119, 71, 218, 1164, 1496, 1817, 51, 39, 210, 36, 3, 19, 540, 232, 22, 141, 617, 84, 290, 80, 46, 207, 411, 150, 29, 38, 46, 172, 85, 194, 39, 261, 543, 897, 624, 18, 212, 416, 127, 931, 19, 4, 63, 96, 12, 101, 418, 16, 140, 230, 460, 538, 19, 27, 88, 612, 1431, 90, 716, 275, 74, 83, 11, 426, 89, 72, 84, 1300, 1706, 814, 221, 132, 40, 102, 34, 868, 975, 1101, 84, 16, 79, 23, 16, 81, 122, 324, 403, 912, 227, 936, 447, 55, 86, 34, 43, 212, 107, 96, 314, 264, 1065, 323, 428, 601, 203, 124, 95, 216, 814, 2906, 654, 820, 2, 301, 112, 176, 213, 71, 87, 96, 202, 35, 10, 2, 41, 17, 84, 221, 736, 820, 214, 11, 60, 760

CIPHER TWO
THE CONTENTS OF THE VAULT

115, 73, 24, 807, 37, 52, 49, 17, 31, 62, 647, 22, 7, 15, 140,
47, 29, 107, 79, 84, 56, 239, 10, 26, 811, 5, 196, 308, 85,
52, 160, 136, 59, 211, 36, 9, 46, 316, 554, 122, 106, 95, 53,
58, 2, 42, 7, 35, 122, 53, 31, 82, 77, 250, 196, 56, 96, 118,
71, 140, 287, 28, 353, 37, 1005, 65, 147, 807, 24, 3, 8, 12,
47, 43, 59, 807, 45, 316, 101, 41, 78, 154, 1005, 122, 138,
191, 16, 77, 49, 102, 57, 72, 34, 73, 85, 35, 371, 59, 196,
81, 92, 191, 106, 273, 60, 394, 620, 270, 220, 106, 388,
287, 63, 3, 6, 191, 122, 43, 234, 400, 106, 290, 314, 47,
48, 81, 96, 26, 115, 92, 158, 191, 110, 77, 85, 197, 46, 10,
113, 140, 353, 48, 120, 106, 2, 607, 61, 420, 811, 29, 125,
14, 20, 37, 105, 28, 248, 16, 159, 7, 35, 19, 301, 125, 110,
486, 287, 98, 117, 511, 62, 51, 220, 37, 113, 140, 807, 138,
540, 8, 44, 287, 388, 117, 18, 79, 344, 34, 20, 59, 511, 548,
107, 603, 220, 7, 66, 154, 41, 20, 50, 6, 575, 122, 154, 248,
110, 61, 52, 33, 30, 5, 38, 8, 14, 84, 57, 540, 217, 115, 71,

29, 84, 63, 43, 131, 29, 138, 47, 73, 239, 540, 52, 53, 79,
118, 51, 44, 63, 196, 12, 239, 112, 3, 49, 79, 353, 105, 56,
371, 557, 211, 505, 125, 360, 133, 143, 101, 15, 284, 540,
252, 14, 205, 140, 344, 26, 811, 138, 115, 48, 73, 34, 205,
316, 607, 63, 220, 7, 52, 150, 44, 52, 16, 40, 37, 158, 807,
37, 121, 12, 95, 10, 15, 35, 12, 131, 62, 115, 102, 807, 49,
53, 135, 138, 30, 31, 62, 67, 41, 85, 63, 10, 106, 807, 138,
8, 113, 20, 32, 33, 37, 353, 287, 140, 47, 85, 50, 37, 49, 47,
64, 6, 7, 71, 33, 4, 43, 47, 63, 1, 27, 600, 208, 230, 15, 191,
246, 85, 94, 511, 2, 270, 20, 39, 7, 33, 44, 22, 40, 7, 10, 3,
811, 106, 44, 486, 230, 353, 211, 200, 31, 10, 38, 140, 297,
61, 603, 320, 302, 666, 287, 2, 44, 33, 32, 511, 548, 10, 6,
250, 557, 246, 53, 37, 52, 83, 47, 320, 38, 33, 807, 7, 44,
30, 31, 250, 10, 15, 35, 106, 160, 113, 31, 102, 406, 230,
540, 320, 29, 66, 33, 101, 807, 138, 301, 316, 353, 320,
220, 37, 52, 28, 540, 320, 33, 8, 48, 107, 50, 811, 7, 2, 113,
73, 16, 125, 11, 110, 67, 102, 807, 33, 59, 81, 158, 38, 43,
581, 138, 19, 85, 400, 38, 43, 77, 14, 27, 8, 47, 138, 63,
140, 44, 35, 22, 177, 106, 250, 314, 217, 2, 10, 7, 1005, 4,
20, 25, 44, 48, 7, 26, 46, 110, 230, 807, 191, 34, 112, 147,
44, 110, 121, 125, 96, 41, 51, 50, 140, 56, 47, 152, 540, 63,
807, 28, 42, 250, 138, 582, 98, 643, 32, 107, 140, 112, 26,
85, 138, 540, 53, 20, 125, 371, 38, 36, 10, 52, 118, 136,
102, 420, 150, 112, 71, 14, 20, 7, 24, 18, 12, 807, 37, 67,
110, 62, 33, 21, 95, 220, 511, 102, 811, 30, 83, 84, 305,

620, 15, 2, 10, 8, 220, 106, 353, 105, 106, 60, 275, 72, 8, 50, 205, 185, 112, 125, 540, 65, 106, 807, 138, 96, 110, 16, 73, 33, 807, 150, 409, 400, 50, 154, 285, 96, 106, 316, 270, 205, 101, 811, 400, 8, 44, 37, 52, 40, 241, 34, 205, 38, 16, 46, 47, 85, 24, 44, 15, 64, 73, 138, 807, 85, 78, 110, 33, 420, 505, 53, 37, 38, 22, 31, 10, 110, 106, 101, 140, 15, 38, 3, 5, 44, 7, 98, 287, 135, 150, 96, 33, 84, 125, 807, 191, 96, 511, 118, 40, 370, 643, 466, 106, 41, 107, 603, 220, 275, 30, 150, 105, 49, 53, 287, 250, 208, 134, 7, 53, 12, 47, 85, 63, 138, 110, 21, 112, 140, 485, 486, 505, 14, 73, 84, 575, 1005, 150, 200, 16, 42, 5, 4, 25, 42, 8, 16, 811, 125, 160, 32, 205, 603, 807, 81, 96, 405, 41, 600, 136, 14, 20, 28, 26, 353, 302, 246, 8, 131, 160, 140, 84, 440, 42, 16, 811, 40, 67, 101, 102, 194, 138, 205, 51, 63, 241, 540, 122, 8, 10, 63, 140, 47, 48, 140, 288

FULL TRANSLATION OF CIPHER TWO, DECIPHERED USING THE U.S. DECLARATION OF INDEPENDENCE

"I have deposited in the county of Bedford, about four miles from Buford's, in an excavation or vault, six feet below the surface of the ground, the following articles, belonging jointly to the parties whose names are given in number three, herewith:

"The first deposit consisted of 1,014 pounds of gold, and 3,812 pounds of silver, deposited Nov. 1819. The second was made Dec. 1821, and consisted of 1,907 pounds of gold, and 1,288 of silver; also jewels, obtained in Saint Louis in exchange for silver to save transportation, and valued at $1,300. The above is securely packed in iron pots, with iron covers. The vault is roughly lined with stone, and the vessels rest on solid stone and are covered with others. Paper number one describes the exact locality of the vault, so that no difficulty will be had in finding it."

CIPHER THREE
NAMES AND RESIDENCES OF BEALE'S MEN

317, 8, 92, 73, 112, 89, 67, 318, 28, 96,107, 41, 631, 78,
146, 397, 118, 98, 114, 246, 348, 116, 74, 88, 12, 65, 32,
14, 81, 19, 76, 121, 216, 85, 33, 66, 15, 108, 68, 77, 43, 24,
122, 96, 117, 36, 211, 301, 15, 44, 11, 46, 89, 18, 136, 68,
317, 28, 90, 82, 304, 71, 43, 221, 198, 176, 310, 319, 81,
99, 264, 380, 56, 37, 319, 2, 44, 53, 28, 44, 75, 98, 102, 37,
85, 107, 117, 64, 88, 136, 48, 151, 99, 175, 89, 315, 326,
78, 96, 214, 218, 311, 43, 89, 51, 90, 75, 128, 96, 33, 28,
103, 84, 65, 26, 41, 246, 84, 270, 98, 116, 32, 59, 74, 66,
69, 240, 15, 8, 121, 20, 77, 89, 31, 11, 106, 81, 191, 224,
328, 18, 75, 52, 82, 117, 201, 39, 23, 217, 27, 21, 84, 35,
54, 109, 128, 49, 77, 88, 1, 81, 217, 64, 55, 83, 116, 251,
269, 311, 96, 54, 32, 120, 18, 132, 102, 219, 211, 84, 150,
219, 275, 312, 64, 10, 106, 87, 75, 47, 21, 29, 37, 81, 44,
18, 126, 115, 132, 160, 181, 203, 76, 81, 299, 314, 337,
351, 96, 11, 28, 97, 318, 238, 106, 24, 93, 3, 19, 17, 26,

60, 73, 88, 14, 126, 138, 234, 286, 297, 321, 365, 264, 19,
22, 84, 56, 107, 98, 123, 111, 214, 136, 7, 33, 45, 40, 13,
28, 46, 42, 107, 196, 227, 344, 198, 203, 247, 116, 19, 8,
212, 230, 31, 6, 328, 65, 48, 52, 59, 41, 122, 33, 117, 11,
18, 25, 71, 36, 45, 83, 76, 89, 92, 31, 65, 70, 83, 96, 27, 33,
44, 50, 61, 24, 112, 136, 149, 176, 180, 194, 143, 171, 205,
296, 87, 12, 44, 51, 89, 98, 34, 41, 208, 173, 66, 9, 35, 16,
95, 8, 113, 175, 90, 56, 203, 19, 177, 183, 206, 157, 200,
218, 260, 291, 305, 618, 951, 320, 18, 124, 78, 65, 19, 32,
124, 48, 53, 57, 84, 96, 207, 244, 66, 82, 119, 71, 11, 86,
77, 213, 54, 82, 316, 245, 303, 86, 97, 106, 212, 18, 37, 15,
81, 89, 16, 7, 81, 39, 96, 14, 43, 216, 118, 29, 55, 109, 136,
172, 213, 64, 8, 227, 304, 611, 221, 364, 819, 375, 128,
296, 1, 18, 53, 76, 10, 15, 23, 19, 71, 84, 120, 134, 66, 73,
89, 96, 230, 48, 77, 26, 101, 127, 936, 218, 439, 178, 171,
61, 226, 313, 215, 102, 18, 167, 262, 114, 218, 66, 59, 48,
27, 19, 13, 82, 48, 162, 119, 34, 127, 139, 34, 128, 129, 74,
63, 120, 11, 54, 61, 73, 92, 180, 66, 75, 101, 124, 265, 89,
96, 126, 274, 896, 917, 434, 461, 235, 890, 312, 413, 328,
381, 96, 105, 217, 66, 118, 22, 77, 64, 42, 12, 7, 55, 24, 83,
67, 97, 109, 121, 135, 181, 203, 219, 228, 256, 21, 34, 77,
319, 374, 382, 675, 684, 717, 864, 203, 4, 18, 92, 16, 63,
82, 22, 46, 55, 69, 74, 112, 134, 186, 175, 119, 213, 416,
312, 343, 264, 119, 186, 218, 343, 417, 845, 951, 124, 209,
49, 617, 856, 924, 936, 72, 19, 28, 11, 35, 42, 40, 66, 85,

94, 112, 65, 82, 115, 119, 236, 244, 186, 172, 112, 85, 6, 56, 38, 44, 85, 72, 32, 47, 63, 96, 124, 217, 314, 319, 221, 644, 817, 821, 934, 922, 416, 975, 10, 22, 18, 46, 137, 181, 101, 39, 86, 103, 116, 138, 164, 212, 218, 296, 815, 380, 412, 460, 495, 675, 820, 952

ABOUT THE AUTHOR

Michael Oechsle (Oh!-shlee) lives in the historic little town of Hillsborough, North Carolina, where he teaches art at an elementary school. When he isn't writing or surrounded by kindergarteners brandishing messy paintbrushes, he can be found photographing treasures like old country stores, kayaking a nearby river, or hiking with his wife and two children in the Appalachian Mountains—where he never passes a cave without looking inside.